Beautiful Scars

Beautiful Scars

NYLAH'S STORY

Lynn Davis

XULON PRESS

Xulon Press
2301 Lucien Way #415
Maitland, FL 32751
407.339.4217
www.xulonpress.com

© 2018 by Lynn Davis

Unless otherwise indicated, Scripture quotations taken from the King James Version (KJV) – *public domain*.

Printed in the United States of America.

ISBN-13: 978-1-54564-264-1

To my daughter, Jan-Rose ,
who has confirmed we wear scars beautifully
after she experienced a traumatic accident

To my sons, Nathaniel and Kenneth
For your never-ending love and support

Acknowledgements

I would like to first acknowledge God in my life, without him I am nothing but with him I am all.

I am indebted to my children, Nathaniel, Kenneth and Jan-Rose for their daily support of my chosen life. Your being who you are helped shape who I am.

A grateful thanks to my family for your undefeated love when I needed it most.

Thanks to my First United Methodist Church family who helped made this dream a reality. Especially Peggy Kroll-Bordewick, who not only proof-read and edited it but also provided valuable advice on the plot. To Pastor Randy for providing the forward to this book. To my many friends and loved ones at FUMC who not only supported me physically but also financially when all felt lost. I could have named each of you but know and love your modesty, so I will refrain for doing so. I am greatly indebted to the work of many.

I am also greatly thankful to the community we found in St. Cloud Region where we now call home. Your acceptance, love and support did not go unnoticed. We are so thankful to be there.

Thanks to Lorna, who made me understand that as "Iron sharpeneth iron; so, a man sharpeneth the countenance of his friend." Proverbs 27:17 (KJV).

To my consultant, editorial, project and publication teams at Salem Arthur Services, without you I could not have done this. Thank you so much for all you do.

Foreword

*A*s a pastor and counselor for over forty years, I have heard many stories from individuals who are seeking healing and meaning for their lives. What I have witnessed in the author's life and in her writing is what so many people seek. It has been my privilege and joy to be one of the companions on her life journey during the past ten years as a pastor and friend. My earliest memory in our relationship is a vivid image of her walking hand-in-hand with her then two small children on their way to our church. It was a hot summer day, they had quite a distance to go, and the sidewalk was alongside a very busy city street named "Division." I was intrigued by this stranger who clearly was not going to allow any barrier or division to stand in the way of what she believed was best for her and her family. My first impression of the author's will to overcome adversity has since proven to be an accurate reflection of her strength of character. This author is indeed a woman of faith who believes that no matter how difficult life becomes, we have the power, with God's help, to choose how best to respond.

It is this essential belief in self-empowerment through faith that guides the author's writing of the story of Nylah. In the story, Nylah struggles not to remain a victim of abuse, dominated by feelings of fear, shame, anger and disillusionment. Reading Nylah's very personal and powerful story provides a unique opportunity for readers to reflect on their own scars from the past and how those scars can be transformed into "the beautiful stories of the present." As Nylah openly addresses her own questions, her own fears and hopes, it reveals for readers important truths related to what it means to be loved and to love others while also loving ourselves. The honesty and courage with which Nylah shares her thoughts and feelings helps connect us to her and to discover again our shared humanity and common need for grace.

When the author shared with me that she had been writing a book, it affirmed what I have learned about her in recent years. Even in the midst of a life full of demands and difficulties, she is creating a new rhythm of life which includes time for reflection, for creativity and self-expression. Writing is a way to honor and share her own story of profound faith in God, love for her children and gratitude for a life of joy and possibility. In writing the story of Nylah the author tells a story not unlike her own. In reading Nylah's story we can discover and embrace the kind of courage and faith which brings healing and hope to us all.

Rev. Randy L. Johnson, M.Div., LMFT
St. Cloud, Minnesota

Table of Contents

Acknowledgements vii

Foreword ix

Chapter 1: The First Scar 1

Chapter 2: Pregnancy, Birth, and Beyond 7

Chapter 3: The Beginning of Things to Come 13

Chapter 4: Broken Yet Hopeful 19

Chapter 5: Sleeping with the Enemy 23

Chapter 6: Pain 29

Chapter 7: The Horrible Truth 37

Chapter 8: Yet Another Scar! 43

Chapter 9: Secrets 49

Chapter 10: Scars Don't Lie 53

Chapter 11: The Trophy Wife 59

Chapter 12: Love on a Budget 67

Chapter 13: Love Lost 75

Chapter 14: Our Legacies 83

Chapter 15: Ugly Truths 91

Chapter 16: Impressionable Moments 99

Chapter 17: The Next Chapter 107

Chapter 18: The Lost Regained 111

Chapter 19: A Celebration of Life 115

Chapter 20: The Romantic Checkpoint. 119

Chapter 21: The Beauty of Scars 127

Chapter 22: Living by Faith 133

Chapter 23: A Ray of Hope. 139

Chapter 24: Matters of the Heart. 147

Chapter 25: The Heart Is Not so Smart. 151

Chapter 26: A New Day Has Dawned 161

CHAPTER 1

The First Scar

"It's a boy!" came the outburst from the nursing sister on duty. Nylah had just had a son at age sixteen. Imagine: at a time when she should be playing seven minutes in heaven or team tag, she would be raising a child. The boy looked beautiful and very eye-catching. As the nurse came for the baby, Nylah gazed into the distance and wondered what the next step would be. She drifted into thoughts of what the future could bring. She gazed out the window; dawn seemed brighter than usual, even though there was turmoil inside her. Bringing a new life into the world was no small matter — at least, not from her perspective. How would she be looked at? People might consider her a wayward girl or consider the baby a hapless mistake.

Will Seth accept his role as a father, or am I just a wishful thinker? After all, Seth, her son's dad, had never tried to

1

contact her after he found out she was pregnant. He left her to live with the guilt and shame all on her own. In fact, he had found it convenient to have one of the popular girls in her school as his girlfriend. Nylah was told about their escapades in nightclubs together. "How can he do that to me?" Nylah had cried aloud. "After all, I was only pleasing him." In this helpless state of mind, Nylah resolved to think less of her predicament and more about the wonderful times she had spent with him.

Nylah's grandmother, Monica, was her very strong pillar of support. She had, in fact, been with her in the hospital for the past two days and would leave only when she needed something to eat. She sat in Nylah's room all through the night and even fell asleep in the arm chair. Nylah looked at her grandmother with great admiration for just being there.

Nylah's mother was far from being supportive. Instead, she had taunted Nylah so badly that her blood pressure had shot up to an off-the-chart level. Grandma Monica was not only strong for Nylah, but for every one of her children and grandchildren. Nylah believed Grandma Monica was never appreciated as she should be. When she was young, she was unable to speak out on her grandmother's behalf. She had made up her young mind to love and cherish her grandmother like no one else had done. She quietly decided, "I will show her the love she deserves."

Then she remembered. "I am old enough to show her love, but see all I have put her through. I am just like all the others, to say the least." She thought of the bad choices that led her to have a baby at age sixteen. Grandma Monica deserved more—at least a granddaughter who would make her happy instead of being stuck at the hospital. She deserved more, but instead got a great-grandson from her not-so-grown granddaughter. Life was a mess.

Nylah's mind drifted back to her current predicament: a baby, an innocent boy, brought into the world. What would become of him? Would he be a ladies' man like his dad, or blinded by love like his mother? Immersed in her thoughts, Nylah was so petrified to think of her predicament that she murmured loudly, "I wish I were dead."

Grandma Monica immediately turned around and asked, "What did you say?" She was pretending not to have heard what Nylah said.

Nylah explained, "Just thinking aloud about a book I read." She melted into her covers.

It was a lame excuse, but Grandma Monica accepted it and continued singing under her breath. She had always been a calm person, regardless of the situation. In all her years, Nylah had never heard her grandmother raise her voice in anger or demean anyone with scorn. Looking at things now, Nylah felt so ashamed of herself that she wished for death. She had brought shame to her family, and especially to her grandmother, who not only was loving, but a pillar of support. Her mother, Molly, had made it all too clear that she was a disgrace to the family. "How can I live with this?" Nylah whispered quietly. She turned to face away from her grandmother as painful tears rolled down her cheeks.

What was hard to understand was how her grandmother, after living a life of great difficulty, could be as sweet as she presently was. In retrospect, it showed that no matter the pressure put on anything sweet, sweet is what will come out. The pressure does not change the nature of the contents of the vessel. Nylah thought, "But I feel so beaten up that I don't know if I will ever bounce back." Her takeaway from her current predicament was achievable. Quietly, she promised herself that in the times of great difficulty, she could remain sweet. It was a choice.

"Nylah!" came the soft voice and a gentle touch from the nurse. She explained that the baby had caused a tear in her vagina that had to be sown and encouraged her to remain calm, saying, "This will hurt only a little bit, but you have been a very strong young woman, so I know you can handle this too."

"Aaah!" Nylah screamed in pain. The pain was unbearable. Nylah fought vigorously to break out of the intense hold of another nurse. She screamed until her lungs could take it no more. When she was hoarse from screaming in pain, it finally ended. She had never felt such pain in her life. "Oh, God, what have I done?" she thought. "How can I go on living after this?"

CHAPTER 2

Pregnancy, Birth, and Beyond

*N*ylah was shaken back to reality by the nurse asking if she wanted to feed the baby. Her initial thought was not to foster any bond with a child because her mother had made clear would be raised by her, yet like every teen, she wanted a bond. "But how can you form a bond when you do not even know who you are?" she quietly scolded herself. "Is it wise to foster this bond and later leave the baby?" After Nylah had found out she was with child, she was told by her mother that the baby would be taken away to be nursed and cared for and that she, Nylah, would be returned to school to right her wrong to society.

Nobody really cared how Nylah felt, nor was there any thought given to her sore heart. She had messed up, and that was it. She could no longer be trusted to make good decisions. She would be told what to do from now on, and she must conform, or she would be setting herself up for more pain. In fact, it was all too clear that her feelings did not matter. She was spoken down to and made to understand that she'd gotten what she was looking for. There was even the suggestion that she had gone out of her way to do this, and it served her right. Molly, Nylah's mom had made it clear that she was not going to ask the boy in question to help, because she had no dealings with him. From her perspective, Nylah should have been wiser, even though she had not been taught to be as wise as everyone expected her to be. Nylah was blamed for everything, even though she had received little or no direction in life. Nylah's true pain came not from the childbirth, but from the way she was being treated. She resented the thought of not having anything to do with her own son, but she had to follow instructions. After all, she had to "drag the family name out of the mud" she had put it in. Imagine: being pregnant at sixteen was dragging the family name into the mud. What would happen if she had killed someone?

Would she then have slaughtered the family's name? No one understood the pressure she was under, and no one cared. Depressed or not did not bother them — all they could think of now was how she would make things right again.

Just then, Grandma Monica came into the room and asked that the baby be given to her. She took him, wrapped him securely in his blanket, and planted a kiss on his forehead. *Oh, Grandma Monica, no one can make the best out of a bad situation like you do*, Nylah thought. Just knowing her son would be well taken care of in her grandmother's arms gave her rest, though that was not enough. *What will life be for this tiny angel?* Nylah asked herself. *After all, it is not his fault.* Then it dawned on her that success was not about money or having it all, but about being happy regardless of one's circumstances. She questioned herself. *Will I ever be happy again?* She moaned not from the physical pain she had suffered from the stiches, but because of the unknown. *Life, oh life, will this scar ever heal, or will it haunt me forever?*

Life has its challenges, but the greatest challenge is having someone to hold your hand during the most difficult times in your life. Scars of the past are what account for the beautiful stories of the present. Later that evening,

Grandma Monica had explained that she wanted to save Nylah from the pain of nursing her child and leaving him behind. She loved not only Nylah but also her baby. But even Grandma Monica did not have a choice in the matter. What Nylah's mother said was final, regardless of what anyone else thought or felt.

The nurses insisted that she wake up at 5 a.m. for a bath. Nylah was still sleepy and begged for some more time to sleep. "Sorry, madam. It is time to wake up. You are no longer a child!" the nurse yelled angrily. At these words, Nylah woke up immediately. They cut through her heart and brought back sad memories and painful tears. Why had she chosen this path of destruction? Was it worth it proving to a man, or rather a boy, that she loved him?

Nylah remembered the days Seth had begged her to let him to make love to her, and she had refused at least for a year. One day, she could resist no longer, especially when he kept reminding her that she had done nothing to prove her love for him. Seth was very skilled with words and had brought her to her knees and made her beg by acting annoyed. Now she could clearly see that it was all just an act, like in the movies. Maybe Seth had even bet with his friends that he would prove his manhood by sleeping with her, because they had all called her "Miss Hard-to-get." It was not impossible, though, because he had slipped off her underpants and forced himself on her, taking her virginity. It was so quick, quicker than even Nylah could recall. These bitter thoughts lingered on.

CHAPTER 3

The Beginning of Things to Come

Nylah's childhood had her mother in the driver's seat. Her father was a strong man, but he did not want to offend or chastise his children. For him, children were his blessing, and he did everything to prove how much he loved them. Seldom would he give them money or boast of fathering them, but his love was unselfish and unspoken. He spent most of his time away from home, but when he was home, he spent the time playing with his kids and their friends. Nylah remembered that one of her sister's friends visited and commented on how they constantly played around with their father. The friend had explained to her sister, "My father would kill me if I talked to him the way you do to yours. I really love the way he plays with you." Thoughts of that moment brought back good memories, confirming that all was not lost. Her father was not there now, but the support he had given her in the past filled her thoughts as she faced her situation.

Unlike Nylah's father, Samael, her mother was in control. For Molly, everything was about her, for her, and with her. You were considered best if you were in her favor. Nylah remembered how her mother had once told her, "Your husband will cheat on you like your father did to me because you refuse to tell me what your father was doing." Nylah was taken aback by those harsh, abrasive words. She did not like to get into the conversations of adults, even if they were her parents. Her older sister, on the other hand, took sides and had decided to tell their mother that a family their dad had taken them to visit was that of his mistress. Now, in this present situation, Nylah realized how true her mother's words had become. She had cursed Nylah, and it had worked.

If only Nylah had proven her love for her mother. It would have been better than proving her love for a boy who did not even know what love was. Her thoughts drifted yet again to how she was looking for love in all the wrong places. Was it love she was looking for, or was it acceptance? Nylah had struggled with acceptance from an early age because she appeared the odd one in the family. Arguably, she was the smartest, but she was also the one with brown hair and brown eyes, so she looked completely different from her siblings. She accepted that she held no special place in the family, according to either her mother or her father. After all, she was the second daughter of three girls and a boy. Nothing special—just another child. "Oh, how I wish life would be better," Nylah mourned. "Imagine all this pain." She sighed very loudly and drifted into another deep sleep. And as she drifted, she acknowledged, "Sleeping is the only thing I am permitted to do now. After all, it lessens the pain."

By age ten, she had given up on having that attention every child wanted from her parents. For her tenth birthday party, her mom insisted that she should be in the kitchen to help prepare the food for the party. She was not inclined to be in the kitchen. To be honest, she never wanted a party; it was forced on her. This made every birthday party feel a little somber. After this party, she had vowed to never celebrate another birthday in her life. On several occasions, she had giggled to herself whenever someone suggested celebrating her birthday. The truth was, she had not dealt with those issues in her life and would not celebrate her birthday again until she turned forty.

Nylah knew she was going to live in hell for a lifetime for the terrible mistake of being pregnant at fifteen. Her life became practically unbearable. Everyone she met or who heard her story underestimated her potential. She was expected to fail, regardless of how hard she tried. She fought hard to keep negative expectations down, and this paid off after many years. Crumbled and tired, she turned the negative expectations into dust that drifted away when she graduated from college. Finally, she had a little leg up. She hoped the bad expectations would go away, and everything would be different every day. Nylah deliberately decided to break the cycle of bad days and live a better today, rather than repeat failures and torments, but again, she sought love and attention in all the wrong places and only found pain. When would she ever be accepted for who she was? This was her heartfelt cry. Would she be ever accepted, or would she have to live life guessing what it felt like to be loved and accepted? Nylah promised herself quietly, "One day, I will find true love, and it will all be over." The scars of the present would one day represent some form of beauty. "After all, the future cannot hold more pain than the past," she challenged herself. What she did not know was that it was only beginning. The scars would one day tell a story, but this scar was only the beginning.

CHAPTER 4

Broken Yet Hopeful

*N*ylah's youth was characterized by hardship far more than her early childhood had been. She had lived with an aunt, Aunt Lulu from her father's side of the family. Her aunt had requested that Nylah live with her after she realized she was not getting any younger and was not as energetic as she used to be. Nylah had just started high school and saw this change as a way to rid herself of some unwanted things in her childhood. *What I know now is that by being myself, I can learn to be the person I want to be. This gives me an opportunity to spend time away from home and find out who I truly am,* Nylah thought to herself.

Unfortunately, it was not so. As a youth, Nylah had thought her life was measured by so many drawbacks in the way she felt about her biological family. Little did she know that it was preparing her for what was to come next. She was treated as a servant instead of a relative. Her aunt's children were all grown and had left home for either marriage or jobs elsewhere. Nylah thought the idea of leaving home was the best way to deal with not quite getting along with her mother. Her thoughts were always filled with exaggerated dreams of how her life would be. She really had a rude awakening when she realized that her deep desires would not become reality.

Nylah's days were long and boring. She had practically no one to play with or to talk to. Her aunt was busy with her own life, and a child added to her household did not change that fact. Aunt Lulu had servants for every aspect in her home. She had a maid, a gardener, a laundry man, a friend and companion, and, worst of all, an unwanted child loitering her home — or at least, that's how Nylah felt.

Her feelings of being a nuisance were born from the thought that no one cared what she did if she served her aunt when her aunt was around. Her aunt was a terrifying monster, very charismatic, and a crowd pleaser. She would not so much as crack a smile when they were alone together. Nylah had always wondered how Aunt Lulu was with her own children. She came to recognize that her aunt was a totally different person when she was with them. Nylah could not believe her eyes every time her aunt joked around with her children on their visits. On several occasions, her aunt had some friends over: busybodies who gossiped about everyone around them. Strangely, Aunt Lulu loved these gossiping hours. She thrived on them; they were her happy hours. It was as if it made her feel whole again, to hear something negative about someone else. At one time, the maid had confided in her and told her the history of the place Nylah now called home. The maid explained that there had been another girl before Nylah, but she had been as feisty as Aunty Lulu. The girl was the child informant; she confided in Aunty Lulu and told her all that happened in her absence. As if that was not enough, she gossiped about Aunt Lulu's companion, totally unfiltered. Of course, Aunt Lulu pretended to support her talk, only to send for her father to take her away when she was found to be pregnant.

There is a lesson to this information, Nylah thought to herself—one she must learn from if she was going to make her stay a memorable one. Nylah had, after all, fallen out with her own mother because of her lack of cooperation in selling out her father.

CHAPTER 5

Sleeping with the Enemy

$\mathcal{N}$ ylah's dream was to be a wife and a full-time mother. She wanted to make things right with her son, by looking for a place called home. Living with her Aunt left no room for the boy. Especially after Aunt Lulu told her there was no room in her house for him because of all Nylah had done to her. Her only option was to look for a man and settle down. And that she did. She got married to a man that did not love her and was resentful to her. She wanted it so badly that it led her down a path she had not anticipated. In her heart, Nylah wondered how she could have let herself go down this sick and painful road again, settling for a life of pain, even with all her experiences. That meant only one thing:

she never learned from the mistakes of the past and thus attracted the wrong sort of people. How could she let this happen? Or did her clothes send out the wrong message? Did her selfless nature indicate that she was less than what she shows? Her thoughts drifted to her first child; her days of pain at the hospital still lingered in her mind.

Looking at her life now, Nylah knew that having a child at an early age was not as bad as sleeping with someone you considered a friend and lover only to realize you were sleeping with the enemy. She compared the two instances to understand how she might have come full circle to the same pain. *Throughout the changing scenes of life, certain things just don't changed?* Did she lack the ability to make smart judgements regarding her life? Comparing the two circumstances that were fifteen years apart made the second one clearly demeaning and unbearable. How could she not have foreseen some of these harsh realities? Probably, Aemon, her husband understood what Nylah wanted and played right along with her, hoping to have the last laugh. She imagined him planning her downfall right under her nose. *Can a fountain give out both sweet and bitter waters at the same time?* Nylah had asked herself. *Or was I so vulnerable as to believe in love again?* He had forcibly made her do things his way without her knowledge or consent, and this did not bother him at all. *Can someone be so devious as to the point of making another person his slave or pawn?* Nylah thought. Had she known, she would have backed out a long time ago. But the deed was already done, and now there was no turning back from that deception. Her current assignment was to live like there was no tomorrow and love until it didn't hurt.

Was it love? Or could someone be so engrossed with evil that the only way out is to make someone who knows nothing of his injustices in life pay for them? Nylah encouraged herself. After all, she went in single-minded and came out with at least two beautiful scars that spoke volumes about her love and integrity.

Nylah was particularly careful not to relive her past, but in moments like these, teenage pregnancy seemed like a much-needed development, even without guidance. Her lack of youthful guidance was not as painful as the lack of ethics and civility she found in her current conditions. The child, after all, marked a period of growth in her life—when she moved from childhood to womanhood. Other people marked that transition differently, with ceremonies and traditional celebrations. Hers was marked by God himself. He transposed her from the girl she was into the woman he wanted her to be: a woman burdened with dreams and aspirations, ready to make a difference in the world. Gaining her womanhood at such a tender age and in an unusual way hurled her into the vibrant personality she now carried. It was a change no one had anticipated.

Evidence of success was her best kept secret. She had gone back to school, achieved her high school diploma, proceeded to college, earned her bachelor's degree, and then came marriage and children. What she had not anticipated was that she would be part of another dangerous plan. This challenge guaranteed her peace and a lifetime of beautiful children. It gave her undisturbed calm and quiet amidst the storms of life. It taught Nylah the most amazing lesson: that pain handled rightly produces invaluable gifts of strength, endurance, compassion, and empathy. Pain was a catalyst she did not want to live in, but with pain came some relief. Her desire was to live free of the pains of this world. Lessons well learned through pain spoke volumes to people about a time when something bad happened, but God brought good out of it. It was a desire to pass on hope to the next generation. The good and bad experiences in life are what have imparted hope for Nylah. Sharing such experiences gives hope and prepares one for the vicissitudes of life.

CHAPTER 6

Pain

*R*eality struck again. Nylah was in bed with the man who had robbed her of her dreams and happiness and, in the process, caused so much pain. Pain in the state of existence she never anticipated, pain in childbirth, pain in hurts, pain in denial, pain of pretenses and torture: pain, pain, pain. It was all pain, and none of it was worth her remembrance. Nylah was afraid to even open her eyes because she could clearly remember that pain of the first scar now. She believed she was too comfortable too soon after all that had happened in the past. And now, almost eighteen years later, she felt anguished like it was yesterday. Why let go of the past when you can relive its hurts and pain in the present? A friend had accused Nylah of being blind to have even considered Aemon, as a boyfriend or husband , let alone a life partner. Not one person had anything pleasant to say about him, but Nylah believed in second chances, and that was what she gave.

Nylah clearly remembered her wedding day: the excitement, the laughter, the music. She thought of how people complemented her on how she looked in her lacy white bridal dress. Some even said she was one of the best-looking brides ever. Her husband was beaming with smiles then and caught his breath as he lifted her veil for the first kiss. How could it have been so wrong and yet felt so right at that time? She thought of how friends and family had rallied around with so much love and support. Her honest anticipation was to live life happily ever after.

The first nightmare started when he insisted that his family must live in their home. His mother, sister, and two brothers lived with them in a two-bedroom apartment. Nylah had never done this with her own family. When she had complained about it, he had just shrugged his shoulders and told her, "They are my family. Where do I send them?"

Nylah could now see why she had questioned it in the first place. Where were they living before she became his wife? After all, that was not the plan. He had promised her a blissful marriage, and not a busy one with all his family living in it. She later found out that it was a ploy to cause her much distress. Nylah succumbed to his pleas because she thought she loved him and would do anything he asked. How stupid she had been because if she had insisted on her own way, the numerous dangers she experienced would never have happened.

Finally, she concluded that it was not love when his younger brother was about to leave for a summer vacation from their town. Nylah was in the first trimester of her second pregnancy. She laid in bed, pretending she was asleep. There was a loud knock on the bedroom door as Aemon got ready for work. It was his brother wanting to say goodbye when he left for his trip. He demanded his bus fare, and Aemon reached for his wallet and gave it to him. Immediately, his brother demanded extra cash for the trolley at the bus station, claiming that his luggage was too heavy for him to carry. Nylah watched all that was happening from the corner of her eye. Surprised, she saw there was only one note left in the wallet, and wondered if her husband would think of her or the baby and what they would need for that day. To her utter surprise, Aemon pulled out the last note and handed it to his brother. Nylah laid motionless, not believing what she'd just witnessed. Then she remembered that the money he was dishing out was never his in the first place. Why did he not consider her or the unborn baby, and for once put her needs ahead of his family's? Where did she go wrong?

Nylah questioned this show of generosity. Did he save some money for her to use, or was he going to allow this little boy to manipulate him and forget about his wife and unborn baby? The latter was what happened. He gave the money to his brother, Abigor, who left merrily.

This really was the first stab. She endured it in silence and from it learned that there were several more to come. Nylah was too stunned to move; she laid in silent anticipation. Aemon, knowing what he had done, snuck out of the room and left quietly for work. Nylah spent the whole day in bed, either from a broken heart or stunned by what she saw. After all, it was her money he was spending because he had not yet received his first salary at the job he had started a week ago, and never gave a second thought to her. He had pleased his brother, and that was it. Did this man really love her? Nylah questioned herself because if he did, why was he placing his family's needs above his unborn baby? Nylah realized it would only get worse from here, and she frantically cried for God's help.

"Love is a feeling you feel when you feel a feeling like you have never felt before." That was her childhood definition of love. But even now, her situation did not look like the feeling you feel when you felt a feeling you have never felt before. *Was I not totally wrapped up in believing he loved me?* Nylah thought. Such an insight was too overwhelming. The man had used not only her foolhardiness against her, but also her chastity. He lacked the capacity to survive as a normal person. Nylah began to notice the difference after she was married. He kept their family struggles purely within the family, and so before her marriage, she had no inkling of the reality that was yet to come. Every family had its own skeletons in the cupboard, but theirs were too unbearable to understand.

"Uncertainty had haunted me for years," Aemon confessed to Nylah one day. Nylah at first did not understand what he sought to redeem so badly. Therefore, like every other woman, she just believed in him. *But is it enough to save him from all the daunting questions he needs answered?* Nylah wondered.

He lived like a snitch around his own home and was constantly plagued with fear of the unknown. He dreaded becoming like his father. Not knowing what next steps, he should take in life. Nylah was now caught between the devil and the deep blue sea. What bothered Nylah the most was the fact that her husband was sinking so low and looking for excuses to do wrong in their marriage. He was constantly investigating what she was up to when he was not around. Nylah learned that he sought to blame her for the lack of peace in their home even though he was sleeping around. Lola, one of their foster daughters, was his little confidant and communicated all that was happening in the home to him with a view to paint Nylah badly. She provided him with up-to-date information. Nylah did not know what she was up to. Lola not having a boyfriend seem to make her believe no one deserved happiness.

Things reached terrible heights before Nylah knew what was happening. Lola conspired to tarnish Nylah's name and was very unkind to Nylah's children. She was so shocked that she stopped arguing to try to fully understand and grasp what her opponent was saying. After all, Nylah had made sacrifices for each one of her children — even those that were not hers biologically. She was stung as though a wasp had stung her. She could neither eat nor sleep. How could someone be so evil as to say wicked things about her? Nylah hoped it was worth it because her mind was made up that the worst was yet to come. Aemon had used so many strategies to demean her, but this beat them all. He portrayed himself as the victim, claiming to have known she was unfaithful in their marriage but was protecting Lola because she had told him. Contrary to his intent and purposes, people knew Nylah so well that they would not believe whatever he said, even if he was breathing fire and brimstone. His story was meant to boast his family image and integrity, which he needed badly. Everyone had known them, and they knew about his parents and their denials and willingness to throw each other under the bus. Nylah worked hard to leave a positive legacy wherever she went. She promised to manage her destiny with the motto, "Truth will prevail." Sometimes when life hits you so hard, it is only the truth that will set you free.

CHAPTER 7

The Horrible Truth

*E*xactly as was expected, Aemon took steps further along the dark way. Nylah's initial thought was not holding him accountable because of his lies. We all make choices in life. Nylah felt sorry for him because he was lost, even if he did not know it. Nonetheless, she swore that her children would never be a part of such history or carry on such horrible accusations. She sought God constantly for redemption for not only herself, but also for her seed. She sought to escape lust and decay. Her silent prayer was to raise her children in the most honest and God-fearing way, knowing that a mother's tender care can cease toward the child she bears; yes, it may, but God loves us, no matter how far gone.

Living this pain was not an easy task for Nylah. Woefully, she counted her sorrows, questioning her own heart and intentions. One thing was clear: God sees and knows the heart, and it is only God that can judge. However, that did not stop Nylah from worrying about the part she played in bringing such damnation on her children. Her only fault was to have loved this man hopelessly and helplessly. He never gave back even a little of what he received.

One eventful night, Aemon came home drunk, banging very hard on the door. She rushed to open the door, as she was worried that something was wrong with him. To her surprise, he was so drunk that he immediately rushed to attack her, believing she had deliberately locked him outside. She tried in vain to explain that the door was not locked but just closed, and that she had been sleeping as usual and had believed he'd had his keys. In response to the explanation, he hit her countless times on her head until she fell to the ground. Before she could get back up, he slapped her again. By then, she had gained awareness of the situation, and she ran back into the bedroom. She headed directly for the closet to hide. This aggravated him so badly that he staggered after her, screaming at the top of his lungs, "Are you packing to leave? I will kill you before you leave me."

Nonetheless, his drunken stupor made him see things differently. He sat on top of her, pinning her to the ground and asking her where she thought she was going. In a weak and trembling voice, Nylah explained that all she was looking for was a place hide. She was so terrified that she was frozen. With the realization that he had behaved badly, he quickly got up, walked out of the room, and headed toward the front door. Nylah heard the door slam shut. Quietly, she arose to her feet to check if the noise had woken up the kids. "Thank God they are still fast asleep." Nylah went back into the closet to hide her already swollen face. She stayed hidden behind the cases, sobbing quietly. She feared that the noise had caught the neighbor's attention, but she pulled herself together when she did not hear a knock. Her immediate reaction was shock, then pain: the pain of shame and the pain of anguish, pain both mental and physical. "Where did I go wrong?" Nylah lamented. "Was I not good enough as a wife?" Warm tears flowed down her cheeks as she thought of how different her life might have been if she had given other suitors the chance to prove their love for her. It was probably karma coming back to haunt her.

Early the next morning, there was a soft knock on the front door. To her utmost surprise, her mother-in-law was standing face to face with her. She was shocked to see Nylah's face all battered and bruised. She gasped for breath and covered her mouth in surprise. "What happened?" she asked as she came into the house. Nylah could not respond and started crying. Based on her reaction, her mother-in-law walked right past her into their bedroom and woke up her son. "What have you done?" she cried. She instantly began weeping as her son jolted back to reality from his sleep. He seemed surprised to see his mother right in front of him. Shaking off sleep, he asked what she was doing at their house so early in the morning. In tears, she explained she had good news and had wanted to share it in person, so she had come to wake them up. As usual, Nylah's husband sat tongue-tied at the edge of the bed, in deep thought. He never said a word. In anger, her mother-in-law stormed out of their house.

Nylah went back to the children's room and laid down quietly. Her husband was still angry and demanded to know why she had contacted his mother. In fear, Nylah explained she had done nothing of the sort. She too was surprised to see her mother-in-law at the front door. He walked right past her and went back to bed. Once, Nylah's aunt visited them at the request of her husband to discuss the failures of their marriage. He spoke long and hard, reliving everything Nylah had done wrong, including what he believed was the wrongful treatment of his mother. This issue had never been brought to Nylah's attention and came as a surprise.

CHAPTER 8

Yet Another Scar!

Yet another scar! "And this time, it is wedged into my heart," Nylah mourned. To have been wounded again by love was a sign of weakness. Nonetheless, what was beautiful about this scar were the two lovely children Nylah bore and swore to raise with love and compassion. She had gone in empty, but was leaving fully satisfied that this pain was not in vain.

This made her husband so mad that he one day confessed that if they were not his children, he would have given them away. "Sometimes, I am so jealous of the love and attention they receive from you that my blood boils," he acknowledged one day. When asked the meaning of such thoughts, he did not care to elaborate. He would still try to hug them on occasion, but was verbally abusive when they did not reciprocate the love. Nylah saw her daughter curl into a ball whenever her dad was mad, and she vowed to protect them from his ugly anger.

Nylah once told him, "Children are children. They are sometimes absorbed with what is right in front of them, so parents should not take it personally." Their dad took it personally and claimed Nylah had poisoned the children's minds against him. She wondered where he had gotten that from.

"Three and five years old. What do they care about their parents' fights?"

Nylah had from time to time referred to her two younger children as scars because of the incisions the doctors made during childbirth. They were both born via caesarean section, and they had asked their mother on countless occasions if they could see the scars. Her children loved looking at the scars and would ask eagerly each time, "Do they hurt?"

When Nylah replied, "No," they would both burst out laughing as if they did not even care if the scars hurt. Children, they are indeed a blessing, and their childlike thoughts helped cradle Nylah's dreams of being a mother to many. They made her cry and laugh at the same time. Nylah knew she was that woman for them; the one who would cry with them and cry for them, the woman who would play with them, yet chastise them. And yet it was that same woman who adored them so much and found every occasion to let them know that they were the best in the whole world.

Nylah thought of her first scar, who was now grown and independent. They had fought countless battles, yet cultivated such great love. He was now a gentleman and spoke of his mother with great adoration. Nylah could have wished for better, but he'd lived with a grand-mother until he was five and then moved on to another grandmother until he was ten. Moving from one home to another was never her intention, but without a home of her own, what could she do? After eleven years of being passed from one home to another, Nylah made a promise to her son to always be there for him. The promise did not sound true because of the past that had challenged him into becoming the man he was today.

Memories of that pain pierced Nylah's fragile heart all over again. She could have lost a son. Her husband was not the same man she thought she had fallen in love with. He'd changed so soon. Within five short years, life seemed like hell. He not only rejected Nylah's family, but also promised to do anything he could to hurt her. Nylah questioned what went wrong. What had she done so wrong that it would make a man hate her so much that he would want to see her down and hurt?

Thoughts of the past kept racing through her mind. She thought of countless instances when her son felt she did not love him enough. Nylah gradually drifted back to reality. She remembered that she was watching a movie. She had completely lost herself in her thoughts. As she walked to another bedroom, she prayed hard that her husband was asleep. Are not husbands supposed to love their wives as Christ loved the church and gave his life for it? Her husband, on the other hand, would claim to be in love with her but still become angry and beat her up. At first Nylah was offended and found no place in her heart to forgive him; then, as usual, she was encouraged to move on in life. She had to let go of her pain and pretend nothing had happened for the sake of the children.

God was her help, and she sought him constantly, especially in moments when the world seemed to fall apart right in front of her. She continually delved into the word of God, seeking answers for her pain and distress. She needed God's wisdom and strength to live through another of these terrifying moments in her life. God was her only solace. Friends cannot be counted on. Her husband would tell her the things she had said to friends because they communicated them right back to him. "Who can I trust?" Nylah asked herself. As she drifted into a deep sleep, she reminded herself of an old Methodist hymn that was on her mind: "His love in times past forbids me to think he will leave me at last in trouble to sink." With a heavy sigh, she exclaimed, "God will do it again!"

CHAPTER 9

Secrets

What would her mother say now? Is it acceptable to make the same mistake twice in life, and this time so huge? Nylah was so overwhelmed with grief that she could not sleep. She shut the Bible and turner off the light but still could not sleep. What had happened to her dream of becoming an important person in her community? She was a pain even to herself. Everything in life seemed to have gone downward on an unpredictable slope. Where had all the joyous moments gone? With her Bible now open again, she read from Galatians 6:9, "And *let us not* be *weary* in well-*doing*: for in due season *we shall reap*, if we faint not … *We will* receive our *harvest* of eternal life at the *right* [or in *due*] *time* if *we* do … So, *let us not* become tired of *doing* good; for *if we do not give up, the time* …." "Why should I not be weary?" Nylah asked herself! "Should I stay under such bondage and one day be beaten to death or driven out of my own house? Or should I stay as a chattel, used and abused?" Nylah pondered on her life issues as she drifted into a deep sleep that seemed to last for eternity.

The lights were turned on. "What are you doing here?" yelled her enraged husband. "I was reading my Bible and I slipped off," Nylah replied. He then walked away. In a state of melancholy, Nylah staggered toward her bedroom, afraid of what would come next. By then her husband had gone to use the bathroom, and she rushed back to bed. As her body touched the bed, many unspoken fears came back. The ice-cold feeling of pain rushed back, this time more intense than the last. An enemy from outside can do us no harm, but one from within knows all the thoughts and intent of your heart and can strike anytime. Again, Nylah tossed and turned in bed. She wanted to go back to sleep before her husband came back from the bathroom. *When will this be over? How will this be over?* was her thought. The sound of heavy raindrops fell against the window. Nylah loved the rain. It gave her some hope, as it washed away so much dirt and decay. Better still, it gave her a sense of newness.

She drifted into yet another daze and fell asleep right next to her tormentor and abuser. Her body was stone cold as he slipped into bed and under the covers they shared. "Please God, take away this pain from my heart. Let my husband understand that I only have love toward him," was Nylah's pleading cry to God.

CHAPTER 10

Scars Don't Lie

ylah woke up to a new day, a new day especially after the rain. She felt a little hope in her heart. Was it all about the rain, or was it God's own way of telling her he is fully in control? As she got ready for work, her thoughts came back to the word "scar." She thought, *I wish I had none,* but immediately changed that thought as she examined how her scars had made her life worthwhile. Scar number one was a showpiece of what man may describe as being still and knowing God is God. Scar number two stood out distinctly as one of God's creative best, and scar number three was one of God's finest masterpieces. These were the story of her children to whom she referred to as scars. The thought of these scars created some peace that transcended understanding. The fun shared with them, the laughter and all the moments of joy they brought, gave joy to Nylah's battered heart.

Her lips formed into a soft smile. It appeared so sweet that the smile widened and increased. Could scars bring so much joy? These were scars that were meant to be hated. How did they come to be so beautiful — marks of womanhood?

As she got ready, Nylah thought of nothing but her beautiful scars — this time, the ones on her body. Though they had ugly deformities, they brought so much joy and peace. The beauty of these scars could brighten anyone's dreams, and yet they were scars. As Nylah applied her makeup, she thought of nothing but her scars. The scars on her belly (stretch marks), the scars of her incisions (stitches from childbirth), and the scars in her heart had produced such strong and vibrant people. They were meant to be scars in her life, yet she had bittersweet feelings.

As she continued getting ready for work, her thoughts drifted to her current situation. *Would it last forever? No, God moves in mysterious ways, his wonders to perform.* Nylah knew beyond a shadow of doubt that God was about to move mysteriously. Or would God let her consciously pay for making the same mistake twice? As she sat on the edge of the bed to put on her shoes, thought of her abuse swirled into her mind. *These are scars also,* but they did not bring any joy to her right now. In fact, physical abuse had been one way he had kept her subdued. She remembered how she was beaten one day after her husband had gone out, and she had texted him to check on his whereabouts because she was about to go to bed. Her text met his fierce anger, and he promised to "discipline" her, as he put it, on his return. In fact, he promised that it would be the last time she checked on his whereabouts when he was out of the house. And he lived up to his promise, beating her disfigured face and then leaving until the following morning. Her rights were violated. Her days were dark. No one fought for her. No one knew of it.

He had his way, and even boasted of it. He promised to do more to instill even greater fear in Nylah. Imagine! For one to brag about the pain one causes another is inappropriate. His angry rage was all too real for her. He constantly threatened her. One such night, when Nylah could no longer handle the threats, she called a prayer partner seeking advice on how it should be handled. Her friend just told her to calm down as she prayed over the phone, asking God to intervene. That night her husband came home, threw all of Nylah's possessions on the ground, and in a wild rage headed for the children's room. In the heat of the moment, Nylah feared he might hurt the children as they laid asleep. So, she literarily dragged them as she dashed for the door with both children in hand, heading straight outside.

That did not stop him. At the realization that she had left the house with the children, he ran outside, demanding that the children be brought back in. Even as Nylah continued running, heading for the gate, he caught up with her and pulled the children from her. Nylah let go of the barely awakened children as they both let out shrieks at being snatched from their mother's arms. This irritated him further. "Ungrateful children!" he exclaimed. Still wanting Nylah to pay for her "misbehavior," as he described it, he pushed the children back outside to their mother, barefooted. The children were very relieved to be returned to their mother, and they held on to her tightly.

"How long will this continue to happen?" were Nylah's cries to God at that moment. "When will you intervene?" she further cried, hoping not to startle the children with her demands. At that very moment, they both reached out and hugged her. Her son reassured her. "It will be okay, mom," came his little six-year-old voice. "It will be okay. God will power you." Nylah could not help but smile, understanding what he meant to say but delighted at his way of putting it. They were out of the house until 2 a.m., when her husband finally decided that he was sorry for them. Nylah took the children straight to bed, knowing they had to be up the next morning for school and needed their beauty sleep. The bedroom was a total mess. As she went around straightening the children's room, they both said, "Mommy, don't leave," as if they had rehearsed it. Nylah assured them that she was with them and was only cleaning up the bits and pieces on the floor. After she was done and the children had fallen asleep again, she was too afraid to go back to the bedroom, so she sat on a chair in their room, where she had rocked them to sleep countless times. "This is my bed for tonight," she murmured as she drifted to sleep, too exhausted to think straight.

Though the world may see these scars and judge them, they are more rewarding after the fact. Clearly these scars do not stay scars forever. "They fester and sow, like a raisin in the sun," per Langston Hughes. But it is in such painful moments that scars are made. These very scars will one day become the pains of the past, yet bring such joy as you think of them. They are visible marks of pain, but beautiful all the same—beautiful scars.

CHAPTER 11

The Trophy Wife

In her life as a wife, Nylah was there to keep the house clean and to bear and rear kids, but above all, to be the public marionette for her husband. When she was pregnant with their first child, Nylah's husband wanted her to be with him at all public functions so he could display his prized possession: the pregnant bride. On several occasions, Nylah would beg her husband to go without her because she could not stand the stares and whispers in the rooms she would walk into. He did not care; to him, it was a sign of his love, and Nylah should just deal with it and not complain. Nylah never thought she was a "trophy wife," but by all definitions she was certainly one. She was the trophy he won based on his charm and good wits.

Word came to Nylah that he had two children—a son and a daughter—from one of his estranged relationships.

He claimed that a girl claimed they'd had two kids, but that was not true. Only years later did Nylah learn that the woman was not insane, as he had made Nylah believe. He had been with Bijoux and promised her marriage after she got pregnant the first time. He convinced Bijoux that it was in her best interest to be close to her mother during childbirth, as she had no one to help her with the baby. He claimed he wanted "what's best for the baby," and Bijoux readily agreed to that. Bijoux heard nothing from him during the months she spent with her mother, and she gave up on him. Quite unimaginably, Bijoux returned to her uncle, where she had come for school. To Bijoux's shock, she realized she had been duped, and he had no intentions of making good on his promise.

In pity, Bijoux believed his "fake tears" and took him back. Lady Ophelia, as Nylah often referred to her, settled back into a relationship with Nylah's husband. Aemon was never seen in public with Bijoux. He only visited her and always suggested that it was in Bijoux's best interests and would be best for her studies. In the meantime, Aemon claimed they had nothing going on between them, but before long, pregnancy number two came. This time, she insisted that he would come along with her to see his son and to formally ask for her hand in marriage. As always, Bijoux believed him. He convinced her that it was wise that both the kids be left with her mother because she was busy with school and he with work and going to college for a second degree.

The disappointment was more excruciating for Bijoux. Aemon never visited her family, nor proposed to her. He only sent a letter to his father suggesting that he might have made a girl pregnant. He explained that he needed his father's help making other arrangements. Lady Ophelia endured the painful criticism of her mum and brother because of a man whom she came to realize did not love her. She endured months and months of pain and agony, and even thought she was losing her mind. That was when he started seeing Nylah and dumped Lady Ophelia, pushing her over the edge. She started acting strangely. Her days were spent thinking of her loss. Finally, she became fit enough to return to school.

Her return was unannounced, and therefore caught Aemon by surprise. He was already in a relationship with Nylah. He painted Lady Ophelia as crazy when she claimed they had two children. He joked about the kids living in the spirit world, because he knew he was not a father. Nylah believed him and clung to him, believing that Lady Ophelia was making a pass at him because he was not interested.

Poor Nylah was now identified as a homewrecker without her even knowing it. This was why Aemon had insisted on visiting her every day instead of having her return the visits. He did not want her "to come looking for him," as he had put it, because he was ready to come look for her. That was all a lie to cover the kind of life he was living. Nylah was the beautiful wife that was meant to be kept at home while he was out scouting through the streets, seeking what was lacking in their relationship: trust. He understood Nylah's values and complimented her many times on them. His first strike was to ensure Nylah believed every word that came out of his mouth. Yet those very words would be used against her. He was crafty and wise in an evil way.

Her marriage showed him as "a user," justifying every word that was spoken against him. He proved to be the opposite of what he pretended to be. "How can I trust anyone after this?" Nylah lamented. She had been warned on countless occasions but thought it was just jealousy. During the early years of their courtship, Aemon protected his interest at all cost. He was on his best behavior. He was always soft spoken, pretending to be kind and thoughtful. He was willing to apologize for offenses he had not even committed. Nylah was confused. She wanted to see the other side, but he played it out very well during their courtship. On several occasions, he caught her starring at him from the side of his eyes and had asked "Why the stares?" Nylah often replied with a grin on her face, "I am looking for the monster people say you are!" They even joked about it on several occasions. Little did Nylah know, it was all hoax, and the day of revealing was on its way.

Nylah was a trophy wife, a symbol of her husband's status in society. Her public life was without blemish. He acted like she was an older woman who had wooed him into marrying her. Her life was a total waste, a sham and undesirable. But he was certainly respected for his choice and status in society, while Nylah died from within. On one occasion, a lady at her church had commented on how much her husband loved her. She had only given a weak smile in return for the untrue complements. "Only if you knew," she groaned in her heart.

It was now evident to Nylah that her husband had watched and followed her during her years in college. They both attended the same college but had nothing to do with each other. It was when they went to work for the same firm that they found each other, or rather he found her and asked her out on a date. She was scared and terrified at first, because she had seen the likes of him and knew something about him from college. But he alleviated all her fears by becoming the nicest man she had ever met. Once before their wedding, he had confessed that his eyes were on her in college, but he knew she would have turned him down. Nylah fell for the very things that she now longed for but lacked. After only a year into the marriage, nothing she did was right. Nylah suddenly became a nag, seeking answers he was neither willing nor ready to give.

For years, she blamed herself for being so ignorant and stupid. She should have seen the red flags but was so busy falling in love that it really did not matter to her. She accepted her fate a long time ago but was not sure what to do to make it change. She prayed for years on end, hoping that the end of her pain was near. She had little or no exposure to the real world or the real people in it. The first time she left home was when she went to college, and even that exposure was limited because she hung out with only her friends and people that looked mostly like her. In fact, in college there were constant complains about her and her friends thinking they were much better than others. That was not true, but they did not know how to relate to the world they now found themselves in. Quite the contrary, they were like watch-dogs for each other and shielded and protected each other from the prying eyes of not only the opposite sex but any form of bully.

Nylah now understood fully what it meant to fail, a concept totally new to her world. Her task now was not to protect her children so much as to make them understand the real world if they were to go to college. Her only hope was trusting God regardless of her circumstances. Even with that in mind, she felt abandoned many times. In an ideal world, her husband was to be blamed for her woes, but in truth, she too should be blamed. She protected him and the marriage so much that he became a mere shell of a husband. He did virtually nothing to help with bills or anything financial in the home. For him, his responsibility was his extended family. His role as a husband or father was to ably represent the family in public and that he did, even though he did not live up to his vows.

His children were there to make him feel special as a man. He even took them to places that were unfit for children. As he explained it, they were his children too, and he was free to do as he desired with them. Nylah was to be blamed; after all, she was not raised that way, so why was she allowing her children to be raised in such a manner? She was an enabler, and that was what she felt she had become. Nylah was to be blamed. She was a hypocrite, and God hates hypocrites. She did not like what was happening but did nothing to change it. Nylah was her husband's ticket to success, the success he yearned so he could prove people wrong.

CHAPTER 12

Love on a Budget

"Mrs. Billards, I would like you to come home during your lunch break to talk about issues regarding your husband," came the voice on the other side of the phone. At first, Nylah could not make out to whom she was talking and was too afraid to ask. "Your husband has asked me to invite you to come home during your lunch break to discuss the state of your marriage, as he will be heading out of town on the next assignment in the morning."

Immediately, Nylah recognized the voice and understood the demands this person was making. *After all these years, he has finally decided to talk to me,* Nylah thought, *And not alone but with the clergyman of our local church.* Her husband knew how much she respected people of God, which was why he had to go through their pastor to make this absurd request. *Foul! Foul play!* Nylah thought. And then in a gentle voice explained, "I am sorry, sir, I cannot come home now. I am on emergency duty today."

The next question came as a shock. "Don't you have a lunch break? You can take time to come home. It is important. Your husband wants to talk to you," he admonished.

Right at that moment, Nylah felt really insulted. *Do they think I can just up and leave my job because my husband asked me to?* It took all the strength Nylah had not to yell back because she knew that was what was expected. And then in a calmer tone, she explained how sorry she was that she could not make the impromptu meeting due to work emergency — as she was on duty for awaiting her boss's return that day. She worked as personal assistant to the director at a manufacturing company. Her boss was out of town and was due to arrive on that day. She had to stay put to ensure he was updated on all that needed to be done whiles he was away. The pastor finally gave in with no further questions and promised to let her husband know.

Husband! The sound of the word "husband" was an insult. After eight years of lying, cheating, and abuse, he was making demands. She was to leave her job, right in the middle of a work day — the only thing she had held onto during her dark days — to meet with him. *This is ridiculous. What does he think of me and our scammed marriage?* Immediately, a sharp pain struck her heart. Was she having a heart attack? It was like a lightning bolt struck her, and he knew how much she was afraid of lightning. He could not even find it in himself to apologize to her for all he had put her through yet was comfortable making demands of her time. The time he never gave her. The time he insisted was too much, so he was taking some for himself. Was it the very time that she had one day told him will tell if he was a good husband or not? Was it the time that had slipped away for eight years, as she had spent time all on her own in the four walls of their home, hoping and praying her situation will turn around? And now, when she was totally used to spending time all alone, he was demanding her time, to talk to her in the presence of someone who did not even know the intricacies of their marriage.

The sharp pain continued. *Oh, my goodness, am I fainting or losing my mind? Does this man think a fool, and if so, why?* Earlier in their marriage, she had been adamant about waiting up for him until early in the morning to demand where he had been. He would come home, drunk and wasted and refuse to explain where he had been, even when she demanded it. In her distress, she called on God day and night to give her the strength she needed for that crisis. Had she known love was on a budget even in a marriage, she would have opted to remain single. But God heard her cries and came to her rescue. She no longer stayed waiting for him but would sleep so peacefully and not even know when he came home. With this lack of worry and attention, her husband became suspicious of her. He still came home late, but he would go around the house making so much noise that she would wake up. Unfortunately for him, she fell right back to sleep after she realized the cause of all the noise. This angered him greatly. He once woke her, demanding that she be up until he came home in case of an emergency. Her honest response was, "Sorry, I am so tired after a day's work and helping the kids with homework that I cannot stay up any later than ten o'clock." She could not help but ask, "Why should you be out so late? Is there anything you do during your late rendezvous that I should be worried about?" The question shocked him, and he did not say anything.

Then the abuse started. He still came home late, but now he turned on their bedroom light, tossed his keys on the table, and grunted and moaned as he took off his shirt and pants. Nylah would wake up, but she would turn around on the bed, bring the covers to her face, and go right back to sleep. After many nights of disrupted sleep, Nylah moved to the guest bedroom on the other side of the house, but she kept her ears open for the cries of her children because they were in the bedroom next to their parent's bedroom. On one occasion, Nylah had heard her son crying. She staggered out of bed to go to him, only to find him in his father's arms, being rocked back to sleep. He must have had a bad dream. Nylah demanded what the problem was. In his daredevil voice, her husband had explained he picked him up to say goodnight. "At two in the morning?" Nylah demanded. She was livid with anger but kindly asked him to lay the boy back down. She knew it was all attention seeking. He wanted to start an argument, shouting that he was their father and therefore saw nothing wrong with picking up his children in the middle of the night. "But at 2 a.m.?" Nylah demanded again. It was unheard of. Had he wanted to say goodnight, he could have been home before the children went to bed at 8:30 pm. Nylah quietly left the room, knowing full well he only wanted to pick a fight with her because she no longer allowed him to affect her negatively. She walked past him and went right back to the guest bedroom and to bed. She went right back to sleep.

Wanting sympathy, her husband told his side of the story. In most cases, people say there are three sides to a story: one from each of the two parties and a third from a neutral perspective. In a bid to make it clear, she herself told her own side of the story — what she had witnessed the night before. He also confided to her cousin issues pertaining to their sex life but failed to mention the issue of infidelity. He recounted that she'd refused him sex, which gave him a reason to cheat and always stay out late. And to further punish him, she had moved to the guest bedroom when he tried to make up with her. Nylah had to tell her side of it all. She explained her need to protect herself from diseases because of his infidelity. It was sad to even talk about her personal life to anyone regardless of their kinship, but she was forced to because of all his lies. His love was on a budget, and it seemed the budget was spent.

To make things worse, her husband also confided in a church friend by explaining all his woes with his wife. Nylah saw the church friend sitting on her husband's lap after service, which was so inappropriate in that setting. The lady in question took it upon herself to chastise

Nylah when she saw her. She further expressed her disappointment that Nylah did not recognize how much her husband loved her. Nylah was so infuriated by the comment that she told the woman to go live with him instead, if she knew so much of how he loved. The truth was that her husband had been professing his love for her in all the wrong places. He claimed he wanted people to make her understand how much he loved her. Here we go again. Love on a budget. Can love be quantified? If so, how much was his love? Not much, Nylah presumed.

CHAPTER 13

Love Lost

$\mathcal{L}$ove can be found and lost. That was the conclusion Nylah made. After all, she did not know what existed between them, and with a history like her husband's, nothing was impossible for him to do. But Nylah's husband's greatest ambition was to put a wedge between her and the entire society. First, he had been confiding in one of her cousins, and now in this lady, who was about the same age as Nylah, never been married, had one child, and was seeking to save a face for herself.

Nylah was amazed at how people are quick to judge and yet consider themselves peacemakers even without knowledge of the truth. As far as she could remember, she was the one who'd been mistreated and beaten, yet she was the one who had to put aside her pride and beg her husband for forgiveness even when she had done nothing wrong. She had not been caught cheating or engaged in illicit relationships outside the marriage. But feeling the need to make things right for her children, she had gone on her knees, pleading with her husband to forgive her for anything she might have done to offend him. Her plea was to forgive her for the sake of their children so they would grow up in a loving home, something she herself could not boast of. Instead, to embarrass her further, he got up and walked away, right in the middle of their conversation. "Was this truly love, or was it a sham from the beginning?" Nylah had asked herself. His behavior toward her hit her right in the gut. She cried herself to sleep because she wanted it to work and was willing to lay aside any differences to make it work. She had met him when he had practically nothing but had supported him in all he did, only to be treated this way in return. Nylah overlooked all their differences with the hope of them carving out a life for themselves and their children. Her children would never understand the true virtues of love, and for this she wept bitterly inside.

A friend one day affirmed that without Nylah, Aemon was not recognized in society. Nylah was immediately reminded of the Scriptures and the character of a virtuous woman. She remembered how during her college years, she prayed that God would make her that woman.

Her thoughts were, *If God has a standard for virtue, then I must seek to achieve it.* Little did she know that her virtue would be called into question when she least expected it. This made Nylah weary because she knew the sacrifices she had made for her family so they could be where they were today. For all their years together, he had never provided money for food, and to crown it all, she had worked all her adult life to keep the home together. Yet, it was all her fault. Had she ensured Aemon provided everything for the home, as so many women did, things would have been a little easier for her. But her real intentions were to help him so that he in turn could look after their family. But that was just a myth. He had acted like he was willing to be helped for the sake of their family, only for her to realize that was another hoax he played on her. His real intentions were to climb up the ladder of success and bite the very hand that fed him. But as Nylah had always said, "Time will tell."

His response to her call that "time will tell" had been, "Time will tell for me too. After all, you have done nothing special for me or my success and because I succeeded on my own merit," he declared to her. He explained that Nylah never once helped him in all his struggles but instead found it convenient to save her money for what she had believed to be more important to her: the children." Nylah was taken aback at first but learned to accept it a part of the challenges in life. His bitterness stemmed from the fact that Nylah was advised by a girlfriend working at the bank to set aside resources for the children. Nylah confided in her husband when the accounts were opened on behalf of the children. Her husband was bitterly against it. He claimed that Nylah was stashing money somewhere even though they were struggling. Nylah took time to explain that before he started working, she brought her paycheck to him for disbursement. But when he got a job, he would not even confide in Nylah how much his paycheck would be at the end of the month. Instead she was constantly informed after the fact. Was saving up for your children's future not in good faith? That was Nylah's question. Love really and truly hurt.

He claimed that monetary matters were of grave concern in the home because Nylah did not talk to him about spending for the kids. Nylah had waved it off as his strategy to keep her under control rather than as a true effort for peace. After all, Nylah had carried the home in the past, without his support. All she had asked for was a workable budget as they had done in the past, but he would not budge. He would not hear of it because, as he explained to her cousin, "He was the man, and he did not want to be told what to do with his money." Nylah then came to realize that she had been used as a pawn in all their life circumstances. He knew he was the man who should not be told what to do with his finances but forgot he was not in control for the better part of their courtship days and the early part of the marriage. Now suddenly, he hated her because she came to realize that she was being played. He had once, in her absence, gone to her office to receive her paycheck on her behalf, and had been told that an authorization had not been signed to the effect. He was so mad that he had reported the matter to their friends and vowed to pay her back. *Does love pay back in the negative?* was the question Nylah pondered in her mind.

The truth of the matter was that "time will tell," Nylah recounted. One of her girlfriends once encouraged her to only wait on time. She used the face of the clock as an analogy of how there is never an end to time. She described the face of the clock as round, and the hands of the clock always goes around. For her it meant only one thing: that there would never be an end to time. It was continuous, but whatever was sown at one time or another always comes back in a matter of time. This means that even when we believe our lives have stopped, the minute hand is still moving and time marches on. Day and night continues, and it is a never-ending cycle; such is life—a never-ending cycle. One man's meat is another man's poison; one man's ex is another man's joy, and so on. To believe that someone would affect your life negatively and get away with it is left to the gift of time, and it will one day tell. Considering all this, Nylah remembered clearly the saying, "Women are like teabags; you never know how strong they are until you put them in hot water." She knew her hot water was very scary and painful, yet it was all those scars the hot water gave her that made her what she was today—a virtuous woman. Nobody defined her but herself, through the leaps and bounds of countless and endless difficulties. Nylah had seen more than she thought she would, yet in all these things, she found in herself a confident woman, destined to do great things. Her love was her greatest tea, hot and tasty. Cheers to all those women who saw life as she did, always willing to take her tea bag and make the strongest tea out of these scars. Love lost can always be found. It may not be found where it was lost, but it is sure to be found. And like the tea bag, Nylah's sense of worth appeared only when hot water was applied. Thus, beauty emerged — one that soothed and claimed the dreams and aspirations of others.

CHAPTER 14

Our Legacies

There are moments in life when you seek to find out who you truly are. The things you love, the relationships you hold dear, and the dreams and aspirations of your life. It is all about the circle of life. A time to eat, a time to sleep, a time to take account of your life, and a time to forgive. It is a circle of life, and for this Nylah was eternally grateful. She had endured so many of these times and seasons. The one thing she did not understand was that she was thirty-five, half of the full seventy, and had not achieved half of her dreams. In fact, she seemed to have thrown off her dreams each time she was in a relationship. She lost herself to any man she dated. Whenever she hoped to move on, she was picking up the pieces of her life. After all, she had been faithful to God and her husband even when he was very condescending to her. Was she going to be a victim of circumstances or the victor of her dreams? After all, she could not let one situation in her life get the better of her because she knew that was what her husband and some friends were aiming at, and she could not allow them to succeed.

How could she now begin to define her life? She had endured a lot of hardship, and a deceptive husband was way too difficult for her to handle. He had absolutely no remorse for the pain and heartache he had caused. In fact, he wanted to take ownership of her achievements, claiming that it was because of his support that she could have made it to the top. He had once claimed to have been the mastermind behind her achieving a graduate degree and a position of recognition. Even though he would not take her out to dinner, for God knows what reason, he saw fit to take her to public events that not only defined his claims of success but also established his bigoted views of his achievement. Nylah had seen it all but had never once thought it would be so degrading. How could a man sleep next to you every day and put together a plan to destroy the very one he depended on to achieve his goal? This was all too confusing for Nylah, especially with the doctor's report.

She had for some time complained about aches and pains but had not really known what to do. She had gone to see her doctor and the claims were that she had too much on her mind. Nylah had always agreed to the fact that she had a lot on her mind, but to think that would affect her body so badly was far from her reality. She had embarked on a mission to find the true cause of all the pain, only to discover the very truth that had been kept from her all these years. Her health was declining because of stress. After she found the truth, she started visiting a counselor, hoping to make sense of her pitiful life. It seemed like a closure would never happen because the pain was fresh every morning. Day after day, Nylah replayed the scenario in her mind and wondered how she could have been such a fool to not pay attention to what was ailing her. But she had been a fool since the inception of this marriage. He had told packs of lies in every sentence he said to Nylah, but this was the greatest lie.

The stakes were high, and her life was like a shadow dream playing out before her. Nylah had carried a slight limp on her right leg. She had done several checks to find out what was happening to her once perfect body. Was she an idiot to have trusted some people with her life? Or was it a defining moment for both her and her children? Ending her life became a possibility in her mind, but how would her children take the pain of losing their mother for reasons they could not understand? One day, Nylah's daughter had found her in their bedroom in tears. She walked into the room and demanded her mother say what was truly the matter. Like all other moments, Nylah could not tell her the truth but only that she was truly tired of the way she was living. She explained that she felt like giving up and checking out of this world to a place of peace. Her daughter, in tears, begged her not to give up. She explained, "There is nothing to life without a mother. You are the only reality in our shattered life. We don't have a dad, and so losing the only person we have would be death to us." Nylah was amazed at how her daughter could be so wise at a tender age. With her voice of reasoning, she had promised her that she would truly think about all they had gone through together and promised to be around if God would keep her.

In Nylah's little mind, it was a challenge to make such a promise, especially going through so much pain. She first felt nasty and unworthy of her children's love for making dumb decisions that were affecting her that day. But in this moment of distress, she thought of how her kids would grow up and probably make the same mistakes because everyone would be too engrossed in their life to give them the attention they deserved. The thought of her children making the same mistakes she made in the past jolted her back to reality. Her greatest mistake had been marrying the man she had married, and she would give her life to ensure that her daughter not live the lie she lived. It was her duty as a mother to protect her children, a luxury she did not have as a child.

With such thoughts, Nylah kicked self-pity and decided to be a woman of integrity. Her duty was to provide guidance to her children and show them the true essence and meaning of love. Love—the all too familiar misrepresented word. Nylah's plan was to put deception to shame and provide a public yet encouraging agenda for love. The agenda of love she would portray was the love that always trusts, always hopes, and always believes. It was the love that never fails. The love that would, with time, define its true purpose and meaning. Nylah's determination was to prove that love was the only foundation any house could be built on. This was the defining moment, one worth remembering, a scar etched so deeply in her heart, and yet depicting so much beauty within.

Nylah told a friend of her pain and the need to talk about it to lay it to rest. That night, she met with her friend at her home. The conversation was difficult, but at the end, she was able to find closure. For hours, she sat in her friend's living room relating her life story since marriage. This was the first time she unburdened her heart to someone. She had been afraid to even talk in case it got back to her husband, who did not take kindly to having his personal life discussed. Nylah's friend fervently promised that anything discussed was strictly confidential, but the friend was not true because she had discussed it with her husband, who saw a need to broker peace. In doing so, he explained something to her husband and judged some of Nylah's behavior. It was a night to be remembered, despite the result. To say least, Nylah was relieved to rid her heart of some of the pain she suffered. She left her friend's home fully charged for the unexpected.

What a disappointment! Her husband got the full extent of her story, and that made him truly mad. That night, he left without saying a word and did not come back until 9 a.m. Nylah cried herself to sleep but then made up her mind to move on with her life. There comes a defining moment in everyone's life, and this was hers. She either had to live in this mess for the rest of her life or find a secure way out. That was the ultimatum her husband gave her. He declared, "We either talk about it now, or we end the marriage." Nylah's immediate impulse was the second option. And strange to her own ears, she said it out loud. His immediate impulse was to slap her across the face as Nylah saw his hand twitch, but instead he walked away. Nylah was not a hero and had no intentions of becoming a hero to save this marriage. He either had to save himself or die the bully he was, and the second seemed his most obvious choice. That was his defining moment, and his choice.

At the beginning of their relationship, he struggled to give in to Nylah, who was as strong-willed as he was. He did not provide when he was supposed to, and she had not bothered to ask. He was contented with who he had become, even with his lack of aspirations and dreams. He was a contented young man who did what he believed he could and did not go beyond anything that challenged him. Nylah did not like what she had become: an angry woman. She knew it was the ugly truth that needed to be set right before it became too late.

CHAPTER 15

Ugly Truths

The ugly truth was her true experience in life, but no one knew the truth about what was happening. Every day, she felt hurt and helpless, but that did not help her. She had turned to the law, only to be called a liar and a cheat. Her experiences of love as a child had been painful. She was taught that love brings out the worst in you, but it was time to do something about it. Nylah's first thought was to seek out love in all its true forms. She had never known love or gotten a real taste of it, but she now wanted to be in control of love for once. Was it truly love or the control she had been complaining about all her life? Well, she determined that she would never know unless she tried it out.

Her first move was seeking someone who really believed he loved her. Well, this did not work out because Lamia, Nylah's friend defined love as something that must be fought for. What? Why should she fight for what should be truly hers? Lamia had asked for her love as a favor to her because her husband was never there. Was he not being cruel too? Why should she make a fool of herself to convince herself that she was in love? That was far from the truth.

Now this was the ugly truth. Nylah had met her husband, Aemon at work and had found him interesting but had not been totally attracted to him. He was used to wrapping women around his finger, but it was not so for Nylah. Their courtship featured a lot of questioning glances and gossip.

Nylah knew she was free to love life, irrespective of what people thought about it and how they were playing things out in the public eye. She was, however, ill-prepared for certain events that would happen. Aemon had an event and needed Nylah to be there with him, but she had other pressing family matters to address. She asked for a raincheck and promised to make it up to him. Aemon was disappointed even though he agreed to the raincheck. Thus, in a bid to make it up to him, Nylah asked him to ask one of their mutual friends, Mallory to be his plus one at the banquet. He said he did not mind taking someone else as long as she agreed to it. That would be one of Nylah's greatest mistakes. Mallory did not only accompany him to the banquet but also invited him in for a night cap after the banquet. Things spiraled out of control only for him to wake up in her bed the next morning, or at least that was what Nylah was later told when she got to know the truth of the matter.

After two years of courtship, Aemon proposed to Nylah and a wedding date was set. During courtship, there were countless rumors about her being a husband-catcher. Then one day, Nylah had a meltdown and told her husband-to-be everything that was said about her because of his lapse in judgement. He pleaded and promised to handle the matter because he obviously knew what was happening and why there were accusations. He addressed the ringleader of the rumors and asked her to please stop all the rumors. Her husband explained, "I don't care what you think of me, but I am very protective of my wife-to-be and would not allow anyone hurt her." True to his word, the rumors stopped. He later explained that he had handled the matter and there was nothing Nylah should be worried about. But apparently it was not so. This very instant came back to bite Nylah on countless occasions.

One such occasion was the wedding of Mallory, the friend that had had a brief encounter with her husband. She found the love of her life and was about to be married. As her contribution to the friend's wedding, Nylah was asked to design the invitation. Her children were even asked to be a part of the wedding entourage. That made Nylah happy, hoping the things of the past were in the past. Unfortunately, some urgent things came up at work, leaving Nylah no alternative but to stop work on the invitation. This was not taken well by other mutual friends especially Portia. Portia accused Nylah of not only boyfriend-stealing but also wanting to destroy Mallory's wedding. It was only after the wedding that Nylah found out what Portia had said about her through one of the other friends in the group. Nylah was so disgusted and hurt.

Nylah was dumbfounded. So, that was what this was all about, stealing her friend's boyfriend when she was the one who suggested that he take her out instead of herself to an event she could not attend. It became clear why Aemon did not want to talk about the instance because of all that had transpired. Nylah seemed to be the problem to their mutual friends. Little did they know that her now-husband had betrayed her trust then. All these years, she carried the pain of not knowing what went wrong between her and her friends only to realize so many years later that Aemon had been the cause. After much hard thought and wrestling with herself, Nylah finally saw the need to talk to two of their other friends about the matter as she wanted to lay it to rest. What an ugly truth! After so many years of pain and heartache, Nylah now knew Aemon was not worth it. The deception, the lies, the story had all boiled down to a moment of reality. And as if that was not enough, the two friends had confided in Nylah that Aemon had been making moves on one of them and had spoken ill of Nylah. What was his problem? All she could see now were the red flags that she had so delicately avoided but that were signals of the truth that was to come.

After this series of events, Nylah proved Aemon was not only a liar but a cheat. After many years of anguish, more news came to Nylah's broken heart. Portia confessed that Aemon called her in the early hours of the morning, asking if he could visit her while Nylah was out of town. In an email, Portia detailed how Aemon was making moves on her and insinuated that Nylah was to be blamed. Nylah was sick to her stomach when she read the email. *So, I should be blamed for my husband's unfaithful behavior?* Nylah thought to herself. *If only Portia knew the hell I am in, she would not point an accusing finger.* Nylah ran into the bathroom at work and closed herself in one of the stalls to cry. Everyone thought the worst of her because of this man. She was going through her own difficulties too but had not dared tell Portia because of the very reason she was now facing. Had she told her friend what she was going through, the friend would have concluded that it served Nylah right for stealing someone else's boyfriend, not knowing it was the other way around. People jumped to conclusions about her life, especially with all the terrible things Aemon was doing. They believed she deserved it and treated her like the culprit. The good thing was that some people believed in her innocence and had been there for her, regardless of what the world thought about her.

Because of this ugly accusation, Nylah forwarded the email to their other friends. Unfortunately, they came down hard on Portia, making it clear to her that that was not the way one friend would treat another. Portia, in turn, apologized and asked that they move forward from their differences. But Nylah did not have the opportunity to let the people know the truth, and that truth is still not known to this day. But Nylah knew the truth. And it was the truth that kept her sane and open, ready to move on in life. Her intent was to let God be God in the matters of her heart. Aemon could continue to wallow in his lies and betrayal, but the truth would one day prevail.

CHAPTER 16

Impressionable Moments

*Y*ears of deceitful happiness and innocence had left Nylah with her own share of men in her life. Some of these experiences left an indelible mark on her life. Nylah thought, *The better you understand and analyze these men, the more prepared you are for what lies ahead.* Her analogy was for the sake of her sanity. It was therapeutic for her to deal with her fair share of disappointments to help her find her way through life's maize. These men were all contributors to her awareness and possible strength, while she took responsibility for every downturn, because she played her own part. She had to do the work required for her to succeed as she defined and analyzed what was right for her. With each of life's lessons, she set the bar higher, knowing what she truly wanted and achieved it.

First was "Mr. Big Stuff" as she called him; his ego ensured he was the center of attention to every woman he dated. And Nylah was no different. He was self-centered and self-loving, like no one she had ever met in her life. Her first child was for Mr. Big Stuff, and as his name indicated, he was all about what he could derive from those around him. "Funny! Isn't it?" Nylah chuckled to herself. An encounter with him was either a disaster or a blessing. Knowing she always saw the glass half full caused her to understand that this challenged encounter was a blessing. Despite the challenges, she was so in love with him that even after her first scar, she still sought him out to make things right with him instead of him making things right with herself. It was love at first sight for her. He literally took her breath away. For the natural eye, it was a chance meeting that somehow turned bad. But for Nylah, then and even sometimes now, it was meant to be.

Mr. Big Stuff had everything working in his favor; looks, education, charisma, and so on. He was fully aware of it and used it to his advantage. Nylah loved him immensely. She even joked and told her friends, "Even if he asked me to bark like a dog or hop on one leg like the girl in 'Coming to America,' I would gladly do it without question." That was how much she loved him. In spite of such love, her greatest lesson in life was grafted around this man. He prided himself on knowing she was so consumed with him that she would do anything to please him. Her number one lesson gained was "the love of oneself." It took Nylah many, many years to hone in on that lesson, but she learned to love herself regardless of what others thought of her. It was her failure to learn this lesson sooner that lead her to the miserable lesson of her marriage. Without the love of oneself, you are bound to allow people to take advantage of you.

Mr. Big Stuff was larger than life — or that was what Nylah's sick love made him to be. During their courtship, he had had numerous streams of women who were either the same age as Nylah or a little older. Of course, he was a little older than her and was very protective of her even though he did not want to settle with her. But they were both young, only in high school, so to settle with her was not an option. Nylah's older sister hated him with a passion and constantly told her she was acting like a fool for being in love with him. That did not help. She wanted him more. Her defense was that her sister did not understand him. But in retrospect, she considered herself a fool — a fool in the most positive light because her desire was to only love him. His failure to love her back only spoke volumes about his inability to love.

The relationship was exciting at the beginning, but it was obvious to all that passionate love declined after a year of dating when she had denied him sex. Nylah was impulsive in this relationship. She sought out adventures and hoped for lifelong experiences. And she got those experiences. It was for this one man she risked her future and ended up alone with a child at an early age. She ignored all the warning signs at the beginning, diving blindly right into danger. He was in a relationship with himself but had an affair with Nylah. No one was to be blamed for her misgivings, misdirection, and misfortune but herself. She was the driver of her life. She sold herself short to the world and paid dearly for that.

Nylah realized that falling in love was too easy for her because love is from the heart and not a rational thing to do. After him, she vowed never to love again, but it was only for a time. She loved the idea of being in a relationship but did not want to carry the burden of love. And so, her next relationship was not truly connected to matters of the heart but one with the full rationale of what love truly meant.

That was evidently so when she met Burp. He bragged so about his eligibility that it left Nylah spellbound. He elaborated on instances of women making a pass at him. This was disgusting for Nylah, yet she played along with his big ego, acting like the pun she was made to be. After several attempts of sleeping with Nylah, Burp realized his moves were futile; in fact, he challenged Nylah that if she was not ready to do as he said, he would rather call it quits and move on with his life. What he did not know was that Nylah had moved on with her a long time ago. After several instances, Nylah made up her mind and promised herself to stir clear off his path.

After several months of avoiding Burp, he finally got the message. During a chance lunch encounter with him, he apologized, saying that he was just joking with her. He had joked about her stiffness on several occasions, calling her old-fashioned. He even suggested that she was bipolar because she would not let him have his way with her. Her initial reaction was to curse him out, but she did not want the friendship to end on sour terms, so she made up her mind to simply give him his space and maintain the peace.

103

In the end, Burp made it clear that he loved Nylah very much and would do anything to keep her. He explained, "I love you, I really do. You are a devoted partner, something difficult to see. I would do anything to have you. You are the ultimate woman a man can be proud of — educated, sexy, funny, and dedicated. I yearn for you from my heart." His confession of love caught her by surprise. She could finally see the truth — that she was worth more than her husband had made her believe. If his plan was to rob her of her confidence, he certainly achieved that. Her plan was now to become whole again, not because she was validated by man but to regain her old self, the one she knew and loved — not at the expense of love or affection but as a true reflection of her inner beauty, her outward resilience and above all her pride as a woman.

Another twist of events came too soon. Nylah was not looking for love, but despite that claim, she ended up in another relationship with Arden. There was another problem of ownership. She did not want to be owned by anyone. She remembered the pain of being owned and was not willing to take a step in that direction. Arden felt very hurt because he had determined to make her his. She obviously had no intention of allowing that. He wanted a proof of her love, which was something Nylah had no intention of giving. He was the one in love, not her. She, in fact, wanted nothing to do with love. He was ready to give up a year-long relationship, all in the name of love. Nylah was not prepared for that, so instead, she made light of his demands. Each time they had the discussion, Nylah would giggle inside. "Do men know what they want, or are they blindly following the next person in line?"

Unfortunately, Arden was caught in his own web of deception and sought ways to keep her at any cost. That she was not prepared for, and sadly, she let him of the hook and went her own way. This relationship was only for a brief period but proved great vulnerability again for Nylah. Had she not ended it when she did, she would have been deep in the woods. Everyone wants to feel loved, and that she received lavishly. Because she was not used to it, she thought it best to cut her losses and leave or risk becoming hurt again. Her decision came with great loss because she missed all the attention and love, but it was for the best.

As always, Nylah moved on with her life. By now she could hardly shed a tear. It was all gone. She remembered some of the debates she had with school friends about the importance of a woman pleasing a man. For her, it was a two-way street — there must be love to give love back in return. That was true with Burp. Another truth was that you can only mean so much to a man for what you bring to the table. Cookies come in all shapes and sizes, but it is a man's love for a woman that makes the cookie totally different. Nylah knew she was not the cookie-cutter kind of woman. She was industrious and loving — two commodities hardly found in the market these days. Nylah used non-constructive coping mechanisms to deal with her own self-betrayal again.

CHAPTER 17

The Next Chapter

Nylah knew that there had to be a next Chapter in her life. She could not sit and allow fate to take possession of her dreams. Alas, she had come face to face with her own reality! Did she need the next Chapter in her life, or was it already too much to continue? But she remembered that failing to write her next Chapter was like giving all who had wanted her downfall the chance to win. She knew she could not allow that. So, she left life to rule her destiny, and that came sooner than she had expected. It was intriguing to see Nylah's face when she was in love again, and this time it came when she least expected it. She had met Bob at an old-school dance years ago. They had exchanged numbers and became friends. Shortly after, Nylah had married, and Bob had moved to another country in search of greener pastures. There he had met his wife. He was happily married and had three beautiful children, but in this perfect family, Bob had felt lost and alone. He searched himself on several occasions to see where he had failed as a man. His search was in vain. Year after year, he and his wife grew poles apart. It was not until after the sixth year of marriage that he found out his wife was in love with someone else. This hurt Bob so badly that he moved out of their home. He decided to strike out on his own to find himself. He was despondent and lonely. The only life he knew was with his family — his wife and children. Living all on his own was more difficult than starting life.

It was in this state of shock and dismay that Bob came to realize that his loneliness had made him lose faith not only in life, but also in women. He would spend hours on his couch watching television, or the television was watching him because he was always half asleep. Then one day, he got a call from an old friend inviting him to one of their old-school dinners and dances evening. At first, he rejected the offer, explaining he would rather stay at home, only to be nudged into attending the dinner and dance the next Saturday. Bob agreed to attend but only because his friend wanted him to. He had planned on sitting in a corner watching the fun during the event. Then came Saturday. Bob got decked out in his tux and headed for the dance. He was barely though the door when he saw a former school mate, someone he had not seen for years — Nylah. Nylah had been dragged to the dance by her former classmates. She was going through a nasty divorce, and her friends wanted to make sure she was okay. Her children were spending the weekend with their father. She would have spent the weekend alone licking her wounds. She agreed to go to the dance with her friend and her husband, but like Bob, she would only sit in the far corner and watch the dance from a distance.

They each came to the dance clouded by their pain of facing their realities. Bob was not interested in talking to anyone other than his friends. He had hoped to go unnoticed during the dance and leave as quietly as he had come, but his friends had other ideas in mind. In fact, they had thought of hooking him up with his friend's wife's cousin. They explained that she was visiting from out of town. Bob enjoyed her company but was already feeling tired of her prying questions. He had explained he was happy as he was, but his best friend had thought he needed a night out to cheer him up. But in fact, he said that his daughter had rightly pointed out to his during her visit, he was always sleeping on the couch. He then came to realize that he had been sleeping his life away in a bid to heal his pain.

Unlike Bob, Nylah's target was to meet someone, play love, make a fool out of him, and move on with her life. Though it sounded so mean and callous, she wanted something to distract her. She was happy to be away from Aemon with all his shenanigans. In circumstances like this he would have asked Nylah for a dance and would prowl across the dance floor with her to show his undying love for his wife. At the end, he would have taken her home, opened the front door to let her in and returned to his car to head for his mistress's home. All of that was over now. Nylah encouraged herself not to dedicate any more of her thoughts and life to a jerk like him. After all, tonight was her night and her hope was that her friend's dream of finding Mr. Right for her would come true.

CHAPTER 18

The Lost Regained

Gaining what had been lost was only a matter of time. The men in Nylah's life taught her the art of true living. Every phase came with a sense of accomplishment, every defeat was a chance to succeed, and every chance strengthened a will to move on. In all, Nylah had set the bar for herself. The experiences, whether good or bad, had made significant contribution to her dreams and aspirations. They were the wind beneath her wings. And now at forty, she was proud and fabulous, wiser than in her twenties, smarter than her thirties, and accomplished by her forties. They are scars of the past, the testaments to her pain and misfortunes, but best of all, to her successes. These beautiful scars left blemishes that could not be altered and that set the bar. She would no longer be taken for granted or treated low because her new identity was founded on God as he uses these beautiful scars.

Nylah wished she had known in her twenties half of what she knew now in her forties. She would have been better prepared, might have responded differently or even better to some of life's challenges. But with life comes growth, and with growth one becomes wiser. So, she had no regrets. She now understood words unsaid as well as those spoken. She could feel the breeze and tell from whence it came. She became better in everything; a better mother, sister, friend, and scholar. And now, she sought the opportunity to be a better wife. It was in her brokenness that she became useful to God and others. These life encounters had developed the person she was, the gold she had presumed to be, the better Nylah she now was.

She felt more like she had in her twenties, but wiser. A set of ideals functions as a code for daily life. Nylah now knew that the extent to which her person was broken was the extent to which she could be used by God. Her expectations were more realistic and achievable. In areas where there was a sharp contrast, these seemed to be more complementary. Nylah trusted her heart, and she weeded and removed whatever did not feel right or good. It was a garden that needed constant tilling and turning over of the soil to bring forth good fruits. It could not be left on its own, or wild things would grow, worms would devour, and scavengers would pick it dry. The constant tilling of her heart was a must — not closing it off as she had attempted to do in the past. With real work came realistic expectations. Nylah had a lot of expectations, but none included a man.

The heart was tricky. It could go in opposing directions from its emotions. This was what happened when Nylah met Bob. It was a coincidence. She remembered she had once told a friend that there was not ounce of love left in her blood or in her heart. The friend laughed, not believing a woman with so much love for life and her children could think that way. Now Nylah was faced with the daily demands of the heart: a warm fuzzy feeling of disdain and love. "Do these two even go together?" she questioned herself. Her friendship with Bob taught her to acknowledge and see things for what they were. No one could be void of love. With a little tending, a little cultivation, one could have a heart worth fighting for. And so, it dawned on her that with the help of the past, she would never fall for the enemy's ploy again.

There were so many things she took for granted in life, and living a lie was one of them. "You never think you will be called out, least of all by your own heart." Nylah exclaimed. She only saw how yielded she was to the process of living a successful life, but success comes in different shapes and sizes, not forgetting context. Forty was the new twenty. Life was worth living — and worth living it right. Her twenties were more about outward presentation, but her forties would be about the inner person. Now, she was determined to show the real Nylah, and to let people to see what she was inside.

CHAPTER 19

A Celebration of Life

It seemed like yesterday when a dear friend told Nylah about someone enquiring into her well-being. Her friend explained, "Nylah must be happy because she seems to be always smiling." This made Nylah smile even more because life was what you made of it—the good, the bad, and the ugly all wrapped up in a snowball. Despite the many challenges one met along the way, there was the need to see the glass as half full instead of half empty. Her thoughts were now re-routed to teaching the sacred lesson of positive thinking. The forties made her understand her potential and the possibility of living a limitless life in Christ.

Sitting in bed one night, Nylah recalled her daughter telling her earlier that day, "Mummy, I am so happy we grew up together." Nylah was taken aback. "Grew together? I was in my thirties when I had you," she replied. Her daughter's response was what had really set her mind in motion. "But mum, you still look like you are in your twenties." In her quiet moments, Nylah understood the value of lessons learned in life and sharing those lessons with her children. She lived for the laughs with them and the mistakes along the way. They understood her faith and even commented on it. Growing up, she had not considered mistakes as a part of life's lessons. The price of her first mistake had almost cost Nylah her life, yet it was all part of growing up. What a relief it was to see life from the other side.

Nylah began to work on the idea of selling one's soul. For most people, it was an extreme action. "Why would someone want to sell their soul?" a friend had asked. She explained that it was offensive to even mention something about selling one's value for another. In her memory, Nylah knew she'd sold her soul for pride, the wanting to be rather than being. She'd sold her soul when she thought she could not live without love. She'd sold the true meaning of life when she'd lived for her husband.

She'd sold her life to her ambitions and dreams because she'd assumed that was what life was about. She'd lost herself and needed someone else to blame. If only she had heeded her grandmother's advice on the value of humility. She had allowed society to define her limitations and possibilities. She was young, beautiful, and smart. She'd wanted to conquer the world, but alas, the world had conquered her instead. She'd become broken from the inside out: broken dreams, broken ambitions, and broken ideals. It was all broken even before she met challenges. Society was biased, and the people living in it were equally as biased without recognizing it. For Nylah, it took a while and a lot of analysis to come to terms with the true meaning of life, and being a woman only added to the brokenness of life.

There comes a time when pain must give way to life, broken dreams to discoveries, and deterrence to accomplishment. In all her forty years, she had never understood life as she did now. Standing up on the inside did not mean being rebellious and aggressive, as it did in her twenties. Instead, it provided a context for strength, an inner confidence that could take her to the finish line. It did not erase the blemishes of the past, but rather gave voice to pain and heartache and streams of courage. It was all about knowing deep down that "through it all, you can stand." Such courage lent credence to God's vision. He did not promise all sunshine. He never said there would be no rain. God only promised that he would be on the scene, no matter the circumstances. Wherever God is, it will be well, for with God, nothing is impossible.

Nylah's newfound ability to understand her true self made her realize that people who lack confidence always believe they are mistreated. It was like being the victim in all circumstances and never the victor. Nylah related to the victim mentality because she witnessed it countless times in her life. There was the tendency to see everyone else's offense but never how wrong you could be. Playing the victim did no one justice. Instead, it took power away. Nylah realized that staying a victim did not help growth or development. It was time to be a victor. Celebrating victories developed character, and character developed inner strength. Being forty not only made Nylah wiser; it brought about a new position of strength, the birth of a new beginning. Nylah looked forward to it with enthusiasm and told the world, "I know I deserve a life but not at the expense of anyone, least of all my children." It was worth celebrating a new vision and a new dream.

CHAPTER 20

The Romantic Checkpoint

*B*ob made it clear that he was in for the romantic ride, but Nylah saw it differently. She was in for the long haul. Could these two opposite views co-exist, or would they need to go on their individual journeys? Bob was a loveable man, easy to please and ready to squeeze. Nylah was also loveable, but had life squeezed out the very juice she once wished to give? To be or not to be; that was the question. Clearly, they both loved life and had been avid friends for years, but was that enough? Bob wanted a casual affair. Nylah knew she was not ready to love again, especially now. Her fears were uprooting those very ideas that had supported her during her life-time of broken dreams. She was not ready to give in to another fear. Could Bob see past her resentment of casual friendliness, or would he, like every other, pretend to be invested only to leave when it became certain she needed him?

Loving Bob totally meant preparing for something new. She was neither willing nor prepared to make this move for a man. There were consequences to every decision, and she knew she had to live with those consequences, but was she prepared for that again? Being pregnant at an early age catapulted her into a womanhood she was not prepared for. Getting married to a man who considered her his most viable option damaged her confidence in a way that made it hard to rebuild. Nylah knew it all from books, videos, and magazines. She had run the experiments from four different angles, and each time come up with the same result. Her resolve was to live with checkpoints, especially in romance.

Despite her decision to slow down, Nylah kept in contact with Bob. He would call whenever he felt like it, and they would chat for hours. These conversations left Nylah feeling spellbound and mesmerized. She got to the point where she looked forward to these calls and thrived on them. She was comfortable with the distance between Bob and herself and promised to keep it that way for as long as it took. The reality of starting a new family was not enticing to Nylah. After all, she had children of her own and was struggling to raise them alone. Her children were her greatest worry because she had to raise them by herself. They were, however, also her greatest source of consolation and encouragement. They had been always there, helping her to move on. They were representative of who she wanted to be and the person she had become.

Bob continued to show concern for both her and her children. What he did not recognize was her need for independence from any man. Like so many other women, Nylah wanted to love but really came to cherish her own space. Bob, on the other hand, was a free thinker. He claimed he knew what he wanted and was hell bent on achieving it. The fact was that he'd embarked on a surprising journey with the hope of taking their relationship to the next level. Nylah was taken aback when he suddenly arrived at her home. The need for a romantic gesture was written all over him. Things went well for a while, but late in the evening, when love desires were aroused, Nylah realized she was not prepared for this romantic encounter. That enraged Bob. He complained of having come a long way to surprise her only to be rejected. Nylah was sad, but there was nothing she could have done to change his views on what he had hoped to achieve.

Now, Bob wanted a family again. Nylah was not ready for a new one. The heart is the hardest area to plough after a season of doubts. Nylah's heart was not pliable as Bob wanted it to be. He had invested in a plan twice only for her to make a mockery of his feelings. What Bob did not know or rather did not want to accept was that she had her own fair share of disappointments and setbacks. Her doubts for every man were real. It was either accept it or reject it. In fact, Nylah no longer knew how to react to advances from the other sex. Her romantic light was gone. Scary as it may sound, it was really true. She had given up hopes of loving again and was not even pretending to look for it. Nylah was constantly criticized for this demeaning look at love. What was hard for the observers to realize was that it was not easy to match her feelings with their expectations. She felt so ashamed of how she had failed in so many areas in her life, most especially with love. A friend once told her it was impossible for Nylah to claim to want a life without love when she loved her children so much. Being in love with one's children was so natural, one that none could resist.

Suffice it to say, Bob was not happy with Nylah, and as he put it, with "the way she treated him" during his visit. For the rest of week, Nylah was guarded about both the present and the future. Must she have a sexual relationship when she was still finding herself? It was not fair. Life had shortchanged her, and she was suffering the consequences. Bob was not happy. He felt rejected. She was just not ready for a relationship yet. How could she explain that to Bob? Bob was now avoiding her. She texted him on several occasions seeking a conversation with him. No response. As always, *Nylah, you have done it again. How can any man love a woman who resists the very art and essence of love?* she thought. In hindsight, that was bound to happen. Love is not about the other person but about yourself. It is only when one agrees to be in love that they are required to make sacrifices. Before then, it is left entirely to the individual to make the decision on being ready or not. She was once again disappointed in herself and was ready to be shamed for it.

Several days went by. Bob was still not picking up or responding to her texts. Her attempts to reach him were not to justify her actions but to establish a line of communication between them. She was letting things go, but not with ease. She felt somehow trapped in her past.

It was hard for her to go into something new without healing the pain. The pain was real, but no one understood or even recognized that it was there. It controlled her life, but she also had to think of her children. After all, they had suffered with her. Her hope was not to take their lives in another painful direction. Her children were only now settling into their new lifestyle: living without a father. To stress them with having a new one was totally out of the question. Men had always been selfish about decisions. The woman was required to risk everything she had because of the love she'd found. Nylah was not prepared to risk her children's sense of stability. If things did not work out after all, what would happen to them? They would lose another father figure. Was it worth the pain again? Not from where she was sitting.

After two weeks of trying to reach Bob, Nylah finally gave up and decided to let him be. Horrible as it was, it was time to move on again. Bob had proved her right. When they do not get what they want, men kick and scream and throw tantrums like children. Bob was throwing a tantrum. Nylah needed to let him be. Finally, one day, after about three weeks, she received a text from Bob that said, "It was so good you stopped me when you did. I have forgiven you for what you did. We cannot remain friends." Nylah was taken aback by the message. She thought she would have the opportunity to explain her side of the matter. It seemed that Bob had made up his mind. Nylah, though feeling miserable, decided to let life take its course. She was at crossroads in her love journey. It was a reality she accepted — or Bob helped her accept it.

The next few days were difficult. Nylah missed talking to Bob and his chuckles on the other side of the phone. She missed all the fun conversations, but it was obvious that those fun days were over. She needed to accept it as her new reality. Bob's mind was made up, and she knew she must respect it. The days were hard. Nylah looked at her phone, expecting a text or two. At night, she laid in bed with the phone, hoping he would change his mind and call. That was not forthcoming, so she decided to move on. It was during such dark moments that Nylah realized how much she had come to love and appreciate Bob's distant presence in her life. He supported her, even though it was short-lived. Nylah came to understand the man she had been visiting with. He was clearly a gentleman at heart and was filled with so much love for her that he would do anything to make her happy. Bob spoke less but acted more. For a moment, Nylah had hoped to love again, but that was all history now. Life must go on.

CHAPTER 21

The Beauty of Scars

"Will I ever laugh again?" Nylah thought to herself. Her pain was so intense that she had given up on being happy again. The shame and pain were all consequences of sin, because it came as a package deal. It was clear that we too often give details to our pain but a shortened version to our joys. Shame is Satan's signature tune for our life. God, on the other hand, does not waste our pain. Sin demands a sacrifice, so he uses the sacrifice of pain for a season to show whose we truly are. Our greatest lessons are learned in pain, when we are misunderstood, misrepresented and often betrayed. Never easy, but always worth it. The best lessons are often discovered during our pain. It was a journey of a self-discovery.

Nylah decided it was time to make life worth her effort and pain. She understood she could not change anyone but herself and her perspective on life. She no longer wanted to be accepted as the victim of circumstances, but as the victor of her emotions. For the first time in so many years, she had found her voice again— her voice to sing, speak, and feel accomplished. The culminating events of her life came with this feeling. Nylah found it strange that she was singing in the shower again, which was something she had not done for the last fourteen years. She remembered how she had sung her lungs out in the shower, only to be told to keep quiet by her aunt. Now she had found that voice again. This time, she promised no one would take it from her.

Destiny was not within anyone's power to change, but hope was. Helping others never turned out the way she intended. She could no longer feel sorry for herself and, in turn, tie people down. She must learn to live again on her own terms. She promised to love the man of the hour and would do anything to have him back in her life, but she must first love herself.

God does not waste pain. He does not waste tears. Nylah had had her fair share of both, and now it was time to rediscover the value of pain. She wanted love again, but this time, it would have to be a love that was worth sharing and keeping. Sometimes we need to open the door to let in fresh air. She discovered she could open the door of her heart again. She was ready to be vulnerable about love again, but this time the main purpose in her life would be to empower herself to express her beauty, elegance, and grace. His role would be to survey their surroundings, determine their course, and guide her gently through the hurdles of life. This guidance could come in different ways, but never by dominating her or forcing her to believe what he believed. After all, nobody can change another except God.

Nylah's mindset was making life for her. Her challenge was that life never works out the way we anticipate it to be. During her life's journey, Nylah had thought it necessary to put integrity above everything else. Her life experiences had paid off. Now she better understood that showing pain, tears, or scars was not a sign of weakness, but a journey to maturity. For many, the road was short. For others, like her, the journey was empty, painful, and lonely. She remembered how in the early years of her marriage, her husband had thought her desire to do what was right was just a public show. He even accused her of pretending to be something she was not. She had believed him. She had thought she was pretending to be something she was not. He once sneaked in quietly on Nylah at work, hoping he would catch her doing something wrong. To his disappointment, he had met her at her office table slaving on the day's work that was to be completed before she left. Her boss was in his own office with his door tightly shut, as he was also busy with his work.

Hypocrisy is the great enemy of integrity. As a youth, Nylah's Aunt Lulu would often remind her that she was evil, but was pretending to be good. Alas! Her pregnancy simply confirmed that she was indeed evil, and she believed it too. She had spent years of her life seeking ways to be a better person. A neighbor affirmed the negative when she would often join others saying things about Nylah. How could one be good in such a deranged setting? *If everyone thinks I am evil, then I must be evil*, Nylah thought to herself. There was too much evidence against her. People were talking. They believed they were in control of her destiny. Nylah was sentenced to pain. She was constantly put down by her aunt, neighbors, friends — even her husband. She believed her worth and value came from these people. If they believed she was not worth it, Nylah believed she was not worth it. There were nights when she cried herself to sleep. Those defining moments were used as discipline and were an application of accountability and a consequence of unwise actions.

Then came the realization: she was not the evil one. People must have seen something in her for them to continually try to make her feel inferior. She realized that if she was against herself, she would always be defeated. Her scars could only produce the best in her. Her heartaches were destined to do great things for her. She realized she did not need people's approval, but God's.

Finally, it was time to rid herself of all the vices in her life. Nylah took inventory of her heart. It was so full of calluses. She had allowed the thoughts and perceptions of others to infiltrate her dreams. "If they think I am nobody, then I am nobody," had been her mantra. Then she realized God had prepared for her an anchor to hold her safe through all life's challenges. This included her thoughts and the moments that scarred her life. Instances of her husband's lack of trust or the neighbor's hypocrisy were clear occasions that need to be forgiven and forgotten. Nylah had to find a way to re-route the negative thoughts that kept her down. She knew she had to love herself: the good, the bad, and the ugly. She knew that by only looking at your weaknesses you are expending energy on an area that may never improve while failing to see the opportunities that are limitless for you. Her greatest task was to see these scars as jumping off points in discovering her strengths. She knew it was time to stop being afraid and start living, even with a callused heart.

Nylah asked herself "What role do I play in the symphony of life? Am I a violin or a viola, or am I just a loud, sounding gong? Sometimes we do not know our roles but we are players in one way or another. We contribute by playing some chords to add to the whole. Can it be walking in love, or do we add every day to our selfish lifestyle? No matter what part we are in the harmony of life, what we play contributes to and adds to the tune." Nylah reminded herself that her heart's chords must be in tune and not in dissonance. Was she walking in love, or was her heart so full of calluses because of the past? She was now thinking a lot more clearly, *I am adding to some form of symphony. If my chords do not chime with the rest of the orchestra, then my life will never chime with happiness.* Finally, she decided to exchange the callused heart for a more harmonious tune, not only for the orchestra of life but also for her very own life. It was time to acknowledge how beautiful these scars were and walk in love to fulfil her destiny — the beauty of scars.

CHAPTER 22

Living by Faith

$\mathcal{S}$ometimes life feels empty. We do not feel the joy of living. But it is in those moments that God carries us. It gives us access into God's presence, a torn veil in the temple of our lives. Nylah knew the only way she would survive all of life's pain was by guarding her heart. She knew that not everyone should have access to her heart, but at the same time, she was constantly accused of being too quick to love and forgive. It was confusing because in living by faith, you need to take a good look at everything that would keep you away from God. Nylah searched the contents of her life but still found herself stuck in the mud. Her final understanding was that God used pain to keep us alive. But the just live by faith. Faith for Nylah was a rare commodity in life but a necessary ingredient to her upbringing. She was taught to believe in God and live a life of faith and love. But the key to understanding faith was to destroy fear. She knew they both could not exist in her life. She saw that in her mother growing up. Her mother was constantly afraid of the unknown, as everyone was, but her fears took her to a whole new level. Her mother was so fearful that Nylah often wondered how faith and fear could be so visible in the same person. Her mother often confused fear with being cautious, but that should not stop us from achieving God's best. At first, Nylah had accepted this fear as a norm in life, only to learn that it often overwhelmed one with sorrow. We cannot hide from the long, loving hands of God because he will expose deeds done in secret. Even our secret fears, God knows. His peace dwells in the hearts of those who receive him by faith. There are four kinds of fear. There is the fear of torment, which exists in our thoughts and emotions There is the fear of poison, created by bitterness and anger, which affects our relationship with everyone and with God. Next, there is the fear of paralysis, of being unable to function. Finally, there is the fear of paranoia, which means to be afraid that others are out to get you. But Nylah knew firsthand that keeping her equilibrium generated the greatest victories, especially with the worst challenges. Her highest highs had been her lowest lows. That was what had defined faith to her. She was often enraged to use faith and fear in the same sentence, but that was how she had lived her life. She understood what it meant to be a giant of faith and at the same time a master of fear. All her childhood dreams were juxtaposed with fear. She knew there were some healthy fears, but her childhood was not characterized by healthy fear — only by the life-consuming ones, even if they spent time in prayer every day.

Her life woes taught her better. "The faith lessons were taught in the wrong season," she would often tell herself. She now understood the grace of God and looked forward to the expectation of God's breakthrough each time she was faced with challenges. In recollection, Nylah remembered how her uncle saw God as a destructive character that would assert his sovereignty when he was provoked. Nylah was accused of doing something bad at home, and in a bid to defend herself, she swore on her faith as a Christian. Her uncle was shattered to hear her speak that way. His view on God made him so afraid that he immediately moved away from her, waiting for God's wrath to fall. God and faith meant something fearful to them all. As an adult, Nylah knew this was unacceptable.

Faith leads us in the way. Nylah came to realize that faith does not make things easy; it just makes them possible. She now held onto that faith that confirmed that for as long as you trust, it will happen. So many friends had made faith look outright impossible for Nylah. She was always considered the one less favored by God, even when they saw her prosper. Nylah wished she had not listened to people rant and rave about their relationship with God because this had affected her so badly that she always thought she was unworthy of good things. Her story was a condemnation to a life of pain. These were the causes for the calluses around her heart. Nylah blamed everyone else for her lack of faith— her mother, her husband, and even her children. But faith is the substance of things hoped for and the evidence of things not seen. Nylah had to understand hope and wait patiently for God to intervene. It would cost a lot, but it was all worth it.

The hallmark of living by faith came when, for the second time, she found herself a single parent alone with her children without a job or resources to keep them. This was a defining moment. She either had to believe and rest from her labor or keep second-guessing herself. Her story needed to be different this time. She needed to jump into the arms of faith and rest there. Was it easy? No, but it was certainly worth it. She understood that living without fear was a fruit of connectivity to God through daily prayer and fellowship. God would not be satisfied until every fear was out of her life. Nylah looked for breakthroughs, but each time she tried fixing things, they fell out of place. Then she decided that instead of being bitter, it was time to grow in faith. Her faith helped her understand that delays were for a reason. It was a time of rest, which Nylah so badly needed if she was to step into God's rest. Her only option was to live by faith. That was when the journey truly began—the journey to freedom, the journey to peace, and the journey to understanding the impossible. It was all summed up in one statement: "The just live by Faith."

CHAPTER 23

A Ray of Hope

"Consider it pure joy when … faced with trials" (James 1:2).

Was there a possibility for joy? Nylah thought. "God is not causing things but allowing them. But why?" she exclaimed. The trials of her life made her who she was today. They consumed her life but always with the possibility of a ray of hope. It was about celebrating life, knowing the storm will always pass over. Her many areas in life gave her the skills required to magically go through life undamaged and pure. It was all about the choices she made. She was bitter and angry at the beginning, but it did not work for her best interest. She could have stayed bitter and unforgiving and developed more calluses around her heart, but what would she achieve?

She might not have felt as accomplished as she now felt. She could not be defined by social norms. She was the outlier in every research. She did not fit into the box.

The combination of both good times and bad helped Nylah understand the need to open her heart again, with no fear, no regret, and no apologies. She was a human sacrifice, one that everyone could relate to. And like all human sacrifices, she was prepared to live up to her calling. She was not in trying to convince anyone of whom she was. She was more than comfortable being who she was destined to be. She lost the dark circles under her eyes that showed signs of lost love. Her cleft chin that once craved attention was once more rounded and satisfied. "No one can predict our future, and none can change it unless we allow them to." Nylah now opened the door to let in fresh air. She could not predict the future but learned that by being true to herself, she could be a better person. Her passions could now be communicated without the fear of being judged wrongly. Regarding love, she did not know if she would get it back, but at least she was not worried about it. She lived by her new motto: "to be real at all times." "Watch out, world, my scars have become beautiful." Nylah told herself daily. They represented marks of excellence and distinction. It was a journey, not a destination, and it was a paradox of how one must live. Life was a road that consisted of twists and turns. The more one drove it, the more one would experience and love it. One might be hit below the belt, one might be thrown off course, but it all would lead one to the destination and dignified end.

In all her experiences, Nylah now understood the difference between being alone and being lonely. One could be lonely and yet not alone. Nylah felt quiet alone in her marriage and knew it robbed her of the joys of living. She was alone and lonely at the same time because even when her husband was around, he was more interested in doing his thing than living a unified life. At the beginning of the marriage, Nylah was delighted to be in her own home after all the neglect she had suffered in her childhood. She thought to herself, *Now this is where I belong, where I will thrive and achieve great things.*

The truth became clear a month into their marriage. Her husband declared she did not chew that way at her aunt's house and therefore could not chew that way in his house. He burst her bubble. She was taken aback. In her reply, she explained her lack of freedom in her aunt's house and the reason why she chose to chew that way in her own home. But that met with stiff resistance. Her husband was angered by her response and made it clear that he expected her to chew the way she chewed at her aunt's. Nylah withdrew as she realized the freedom she thought she had gained was not real. She was going to be living with a lord and master who would even want to guide her chewing skills. She thought, *"Oh my God, what have I gotten myself into?* This question rang in Nylah's mind for days on end. She now knew that there were certain expectations she would be required to live by as his wife. This immediately suggested that Nylah lose her identity by forgetting what she was and what she loved.

Twelve years into the marriage, she realized she had indeed lost herself to someone who really did not care. She watched movies he or the children loved; she ate meals only he or the children wanted. She stopped living for herself and just lived for them. Nylah realized that her husband was at peace with himself. His desire was the to scare the life out of her, and that was exactly what he achieved. She was never real, always pretending to like what she did not like and being treated like a second-class citizen in her own home. Yes, he considered himself a husband, which for many men meant he was her lord. But he was expected to love her like his own body if she was to honor him too. But that was not the case; Nylah was just a door rug that would tend to the needs of both her husband and children. It was the life she dreaded, and she could not believe it was truly hers. She gave up on all hopes of living her dreams. Now her dreams did not matter. It was either his or none. It was his wife's duty to ensure the kids where in school when they were supposed to be in school regardless of how she felt. Her husband had made it clear that because she worked, it was her duty to tend to the children. His was to take care of his extended family as he had promised them. Nylah's life was all a lie. This was not what she had bargained for. To care for the home and children, she promised herself she would do, but to see to his needs was totally out of the question.

The abuse was far more than she could handle. Now as Nylah looked back, she could not tell how she had survived. But she had learned to live all over again. She now sang in the shower, after she had lost the ability to even sing, let alone in the shower. Nylah had a great voice. As a child, she would sit by the radio and act like the songs were coming from it while she sang. One day, her sister had come running from her room to listen to a song on the radio only to realize it was Nylah singing. She was truly annoyed. For Nylah, it was a great indication that one day she would sing; to have pretended and still sounded so good meant she had a lot to give. Living with her aunt, Nylah could only sing in the shower, and even then, she was constantly asked to stop making noise. She had no choice but to do as she was told. When Nylah finally made it to college, she found a group of singers and became a part of them. Her friends would laugh at her voice when she sang because it was not trained and came out loud and obnoxious. Nylah laughed with them but found it wonderful that she could sing without being told to keep quiet. With that atmosphere of encouragement, Nylah practiced her music and did her songs all on her own, especially when her roommate went home for weekends. She, unlike many of the other girls, did not go home for weekends because she was afraid of what her aunt had in store for her. Nylah stayed in her college room on weekends and practiced endlessly. This paid off, and by the time Nylah had completed college, her singing abilities had increased, and so had her confidence.

But she lost it all during her marriage. After the children came, her husband made it clear that she had to stay home after work to tend to the needs of the children. She was crushed but loved her children too much to sacrifice their lives. It became the norm that she went to work and came straight home to tend to the children. No longer was she to engage in musicals and other festive renditions. She had to be home with the children; that was her duty. After twelve years of losing herself to the children and home affairs, Nylah was liberated by the divorce settlement. For the first time, she lived her life, ate what she wanted, sang in as many groups as she could, but was still mindful of raising the children. She promoted her children's abilities, and when the time had fully come, she started all over again. It was hard, but Nylah was thankful again to do what she loved the most: sing. Finding her voice gave her a ray of hope that one day she would find herself again. It was a journey of a lifetime, but there was a ray of hope.

CHAPTER 24

Matters of the Heart

"I feel like I am dying. My career, my marriage, my education, my life — oh my life — it is all crumbling right in front of me, and there is nothing I can do." Nylah remembered these words so clearly. Her heart had stopped beating, but she was not dead. "Why am I not dead?" she asked, "Oh why? I am like a walking nightmare...." Matters of the heart are so hard to handle. Yet, many would have thought it wise to stay undecided after all the heart-aches and broken dreams. Who was she living for? One of her sons told her he never felt loved. Her husband did not even take a second look at her. And her career was another sham; she was asked to begin all over again, like she had never even started. She was so angry with life, yet she had

her children who did not know what was happening. She
cried in the privacy of her bedroom, but even there she
was never alone. Her children would burst in at any time.
Then she had to quickly dry her eyes or they would ask,
"Why are you crying, Mama? Are we being bad, or is dad
being mean again?" Strangely, the children understood
the constant argument in the home, and this made them
uncomfortable. They were not too young to understand
that their dad was being mean, but they did not know to
what extent. Nylah promised to protect them. It was only
because of them that she knew she could not die. For their
sake, dying was not an option—but what was?

Nylah knew she had to reinvent herself. She did not
know how, only that she had to do so. Then came the
breakthrough. She had to decide to shake free from all
the oppression. One thing led to another. Getting out of
bed was the first step toward victory. How she hated getting out of bed! It was a sorry reminder of the life she
never chose. The next step was to appreciate every little
thing that had made her who she was. Her thoughts were,
*I can either consider these challenges burdens or stepping
stones.* It became clearer when she realized she could be
living with so many blessings yet not even see them. Her
thoughts were either her greatest ally or enemy. Every

step depended on her thought process. How she viewed the world was how the world would be. It was time for the breakthrough. She started living her truth. Your past is not what you are; your present is a gift, and your future is the dreams and aspiration in motion.

Nylah had a clearer vision of what life ought to be. She had loved and lost, but after connecting the dots of her life, she knew there needed to be rebirth. She found herself again. She had never thought she would be lost in life, yet she was lost for an entire decade—an entire decade! Life worries had made it feel a lot more. Nylah thought of finding her way and becoming the person she had always wanted to be. She was a woman on her own, the woman God had destined her to be: a woman of substance. She could not allow any negative breaks to take that away from her. And years of hardship and pain had taught her that she needed to live again.

Nylah always loved family. It gave her a sense of security. But instead, life taught her that there was only one way to be secure, and that was in God and herself, not in someone else. She was a woman of big dreams—dreams of what the world could be—but Nylah knew that a rebirth of self was the only way she could achieve her dreams. This was a serious matter because it dealt with the heart. Life was what she could accomplish with God on her side and on her own, more so than what someone else can do for her. She knew she had to believe in herself again. Her confidence had waned, but she knew she must rekindle the fire that made her the woman the world had seen.

In her journey of rebirth, Nylah read of women in the Bible who found themselves against all odds. She read of historical events that had put women on the scene. Her plan was to see what she had in common with such women, then take it to the next level. After much reading, it became clear that men who were not too sure of themselves found it easier to latch onto a woman with strength. By doing so, they not only found a convenient spot to shine, but in the process sought ways to downplay the woman's strength. That was what her ex-husband had done. Now, she knew it had nothing to do with her lack of wisdom or strength. It was about his playing with her mind. Yes, he succeeded for a while, but when it came to matters of the heart, strength is strength. No matter what, it was her God-given right to be free from guilt, condemnation, and fear of failure. Nylah had the right to be free, and while becoming free from within, she started a whole new journey of fulfilment. Awakened emotion meant movement because it was from the heart.

CHAPTER 25

The Heart
Is Not so Smart

*I*t happened suddenly! Freedom was restored and so was the desire to live again. Nylah, wanted to live again. In her season of loneliness and pain, she had made the most of her time. She had resisted the temptation to do nothing and thought of creative ways to take advantage of this season in her life. It was during this season that she classified the kinds of people one might meet in one's journey through life. She remembered her sister constantly telling her of the different kinds of people in life. "Some people come for a reason, others for a season, while others for a lifetime." Her sister would say. "God's ways are not our ways."

In this season of reprogramming, Nylah knew faith would begin by shifting her thoughts. There were thoughts of good as God intended and not of evil to bring her to her expected end. This season was designed to burn away her insecurities. In doing that, she became aware of five categories of people she met along the way: party poopers, willy dillies, project partners, dream killers, and the gossip. For Nylah, each of these groups of people served a purpose in her life. Her responsibility was now to understand the pain each category contributed and to be able to forgive. Identifying the challenge means acknowledging the reality of the situation, forgiving, and learning to let go. To move on, she had to forgive all, with or without acknowledgement or answerability.

To identify these categories meant doing the work and eagerly wanting to reap the benefits of forgiveness. As she named them, she diminished the power or control each group had over her, not falling into any order of relevance as the pain subsided.

Party Poopers

Misery loves company. People in this category are often close acquaintances who can either speak life or death into your circumstances. Their tasks vary from either adulteration of fun or lack of participation. It is at times, easy to spot them everywhere, but in other cases, you have to be gifted to discern their intent. It was apparent that family members rank first in this category. You are not allowed to be happy if they are not happy. It took Nylah years to be able to identify that they were sucking the life from her when they interjected a sarcastic comment or choose to be downright nasty. At first, they just rubbed her the wrong way. With time, Nylah became less bothered by their intentions. It became a little easier to ignore them and move on.

Willy Dillies

Unlike party poopers, willy dillies own a special place on the chart. These are attention-deprived people. They were either deprived of attention as a child or did not have someone who really cared. Nylah's first encounter with a willy dilly was through a neighborhood friend called Delta. Delta was an attention whore. Growing up, Delta never liked Nylah. She showed her disdain in so many ways. In Delta's eyes, Nylah got too much point-less attention; who was she after all? What Delta did not know or understand was the depth of Nylah's struggles that had orchestrated her need for success. All Delta saw was the glam and the glitz, as this negates the struggles and pains.

Delta loaned some money to Nylah and was late to pay it back. Delta dissed Nylah to everyone who would listen. Delta complained that her good faith and help was not given the importance she had anticipated. The hostility dragged on for months, and Delta became more vicious with her words. Finally, Nylah paid back the money she owed. She decided from then on that help from God was the only help she would accept. These were long, painful nights for Nylah. She learned her lesson the hard way. Eventually, she and Delta talked about it, and she moved on. Some lessons are meant for a lifetime. Help from a friend is never commensurate with waiting on God.

Project Partners

Ironically, project partners are ubiquitous. Diligent though they might appear, their real intent is to develop the project and move on after completion with no affection or affirmation. The eminent threat from this group is when the project seems to get all the attention. How someone could be helped so they looked better is normally the question. The project under construction needs to be under strict scrutiny. The subject is judged by appearance, not reality. This was how Nylah felt when she received help from a friend. She was constantly judged by how she appeared instead of by what was truly happening. Should there be any semblance of normalcy, the subject under scrutiny might no longer be qualified for support. You are no longer their friends. Nylah did not understand the depth of project partners until she met one, someone she had helped in the past. Bellay, a former schoolmate and friend, was in trouble and needed someone to talk to. She found Nylah, and they hit it off. Nylah readily offered Bellay a shoulder to cry on, in the spirit of true friendship. Bellay confided totally in Nylah and emptied out her heart. Nylah lived up to the girl code and was there through thick and thin. She did not criticize or condemn Bellay for her misfortunes. On the contrary, she urged her to move on and forget the past.

Then it all changed. Bellay's planned visit brought out a side of her that Nylah never knew existed. Nylah's once chaotic life had dramatically turned for the better. Nylah looked too comfortable for Bellay. Bellay thought she was going to see things fall apart in Nylah's life. Nylah seemed a lot more put together than she had expected. However, from Bellay's eyes, Nylah saw that she did not like what had become of her friend. Nothing was spoken, but the unspoken words are the diabolic ones. Upon her return home, things shifted. Bellay did not call as she used to. In one of their far and few in between conversations, Bellay expressed her dissatisfaction with taking care of everyone else but herself. To make matters worse, she only called when she was about to travel and needed some money to meet her travelling expenses. It was hard at first for Nylah to accept the change. Nylah was lost for a while, but knew she had to make a choice: to be either right about what she had seen in Bellay or to be happy. For obvious reasons, she chose the latter. Her promise was to endure hardship like a good soldier of God because it was only by grace anyone could stand.

Dream Killers

> Keep thy heart with all diligence; for out of
> it are the issues of life (Proverbs 4: 23).

Nylah saw this reading from a working woman website:

The older I get, the more I realize the value
of privacy, of cultivating your circle and
only letting certain people in. You can be
open, honest, and real while still understanding not everyone deserves a seat at
the table of your life.

Nylah knew this to be true but sometimes allowed
people into her life as a communicator. Being discrete,
especially when in pain, is a necessity of life. Some people
can hug you but still not stand you. That's okay because
your purpose is not in the hands of man. Your silence can
be your sermon. Nylah had to learn this the hard way.
She concluded that not everyone was cut out for understanding her dreams.

Nylah knew she had to be careful of dream killers,
because there are so many of them lurking around. The
trick is the less they know, the more you have power and
control over your own dreams.

Gossipers

The greatest lessons of Jesus's teachings are the things
he did not say. The Bible tells us to be slow to speak and

quick to listen. Suffice to say, that is not so for gossipers. Silence is better than response, but not for these people. Like the Pharisees, they weaponize their words to those we love. Words are like seeds: they germinate and grow and sometimes end up as mighty oaks. People constantly target others when they do not feel secure themselves. Gossipers are no exception. They would say any and everything, totally not their business, in the guise of wanting to help. They believe they know the truth, even when it does not concern them.

Nylah had kept some parts of her life a secret from her sister. It was a temporary fix to help her see life on the other side and keep her sister from following in Nylah's footsteps.

Evidently, a friend called Eric Sheldon was desperate to make Nylah admit to her mistake. He thought telling on Nylah was a start on the punishment she should have received a long time ago. Eric told Violet, Nylah's sister, about Nylah's baby. This incident caused a rift in the family. Violet's reaction was wild. She confronted Nylah, seeking to know why such an important information had been kept from her. Nylah was at a loss for words. After a few hours of hard words, Violet finally accepted Nylah's explanation as to the why she was not told. Unfortunately, years after, Violet fell a prey to the same experiences as Nylah. To this day, Violet struggles with her children. Her marriage has fallen apart, and she is still grasping straws in her life.

Nylah blamed herself for years. Thanks to Eric, her sister had to live through the same pain Nylah endured. Gossipers cannot be trusted. Nylah blamed herself, but the true culprit was Eric. Had he minded his own business, things could have been a lot different. Now Nylah was left to pick up the pieces of their broken lives, especially that of her sister, who was not as strong as Nylah was.

It was amazing to see how far she had come with these five kinds of people riding along. Nylah knew it was no longer necessary to negotiate with people about her life. Her goal was to forgive herself and everyone else who in some way or another caused her pain. It was time to move on to the next Chapter. A new day had dawned.

CHAPTER 26

A New Day Has Dawned

With obedience came deliverance. Nylah knew she had to obey and forgive. "I forgive you" — there is a lot of power in those three words. Nylah knew a new day had dawned. She understood you cannot hide from the long, loving hand of God for long. She had been hiding long enough. Now it was a new day. Her heart was more tender and loving, no longer holding people hostage because of hurts. The lesson was to "let it go and let God" — the good, the bad, and the ugly. It was time to make something beautiful of those messed up scars and broken dreams. Now it was time to recognize them, acknowledge them, and use them for the greater good. There was no need to take these scars of the past and make them her reality. These scars of the past are truly beautiful. It was only in accepting and living with them that her true beauty came.

These beautiful scars made her who she was. Scars from childbirth, from betrayal, from broken hearts and broken dreams, scars of lessons learned, and rejection felt. It was time to celebrate these beautiful scars, for they were stories of being loved and lost. Scars remind us of our life's journey — where we have been, what we have become, and where we hope to be. Scars never dictate our life's journey unless we let them. They prepared Nylah for her future. "I can't allow them to order my future," exclaimed Nylah, "I have the power to make it work… such Beautiful Scars."

CPSIA information can be obtained
at www.ICGtesting.com
Printed in the USA
LVHW010742281118
598386LV00002B/128